Maureen Duffy was born in Worthing, Sussex, in 1933 and took her degree in English at King's College, London in 1956. She was a schoolteacher for five years, and in 1962 she published her first novel, *That's How It Was*, which won her immediate acclaim. Since then she has published twelve novels, four volumes of verse, a biography of Aphra Behn, a social history, an animal rights handbook and had six plays performed.

Love Child, first published in 1971, is one of the finest novels by one of our most consistently exciting and impressive contemporary writers.

Alison Hennegan, the series editor of *Lesbian Landmarks*, read English at Girton College, Cambridge. From 1977 until its closure in 1983 she was Literary Editor and Assistant Features Editor at *Gay News*. She went on to become Editor of The Women's Press Bookclub 1984–1991 and in 1992 launched the specialist feminist Open Letters Bookclub, which she currently edits.

LESBIAN LANDMARKS

Lesbian writing is booming today – from the most rigorous of scholarly studies to the softest of soft-centre fiction – with special lesbian sections in many bookshops, crammed with volumes from the tiniest lesbian presses and the biggest publishing giants. In the midst of such plenty, it's easy to forget that it was not always so . . . .

Lesbian Landmarks is an exciting new series of reprints which illuminates the rich and eventful history of lesbian writing.

Their politics as varied as their prose and poetry, their ideas on gender as diverse as the genres in which they express them, the writers reprinted here span centuries, castes and cultures. Some were celebrated in their lifetimes but are now forgotten; others were silenced and exiled.

Amongst these authors you will find remarkable innovators in style and content. You may also find women whose far distant attitudes and assumptions perplex or even anger you. But all of them, in their different ways, engaged in the long struggle to articulate and explore ways of living and loving that have, over the centuries, been variously misrepresented, feared, pathologized and outlawed.

The world these authors knew was often a world apart from ours; yet however unlikely it may sometimes seem, each of these books has helped to make possible today's frequently very different, confidently open lesbian writing. These, in short, are Lesbian Landmarks.

Maureen
Duffy

Love Child

Introduction by Alison Hennegan

Published by VIRAGO PRESS Limited, March 1994
42–43 Gloucester Crescent, London NW1 7PD

First published in Great Britain by Weidenfeld & Nicolson 1971

Printed and bound in Great Britain by
Cox & Wyman Ltd, Reading, Berks

For St. Venus

"And Queens hereafter shall
be glad to live
Upon the alms of thy
superfluous praise."

Introduction

'If I don't feel myself greatly my parents' child I do, maybe more so because of that, feel myself the inheritor of civilization'

Rather risibly grandiose words perhaps from a young teenager. Yet Kit, the narrator of *Love Child* who utters them, is the extraordinary child of extraordinary parents who have endorsed their offspring with the rich, full fruits of their own impressively wide ranging knowledge. As Kit goes on to explain:

> My imagination is stuffed with the legends of the world, mainly the Western world of course though the East has given its share too in Babylon and China and, by extension, Mohawk and Apache and Christian myth, like a pirates' hoard of Arabian nights' treasure. At any moment I can open my store and gloat in secret over its jewels and time-untarnished finery. I find them more evocative than the synthetic *diamanté* of our own time; war heroes and movie stars acting out the same legends I have observed on some great canvas in the Prado or heard at La Scala.

So wide a range of cultural reference is only to be

expected from a family such as Kit's. Their many households – including those in London, America, Scandinavia and Italy – are cosmopolitan to say the least. An English, more or less, mother, a Scandiwegian husband, and Kit, their precocious only child, can between them muster seven dead languages and five living, 'apart from ubiquitous English and smatterings of Cantonese, Urdu and Yoruba picked up on my father's travels. Foreign doesn't exist for us as a concept.' And neither does Home. 'We', as Kit explains to the reader, 'are international. We do not belong to any one place or sometimes I think even to any one time. Where we were born is irrelevant.' 'That's right; that's how it ought to be', Kit is told later in the book by Leo, an American draft-dodger seeking temporary refuge on the beach of the tiny Italian fishing village where Kit's family is, as usual, spending the summer.

It sounds perfect: true Citizens of the World! How splendidly universal, how gloriously free from insularity, parochial vision and aggressive tribal emotions. But to make the world so very much one's oyster brings its own perils. For Kit, being 'a citizen of the world' entails being an eternally displaced person, one not even truly at home in what might seem to be a native language. Kit's own English is an uneasy mosaic: there is the elegantly formal, just very slightly dated language in which the bulk of *Love Child* is narrated; there are occasional, in the context jarring, Americanisms, to remind us that a Massachusetts farm is one of the family 'homes' and that amongst the clutch of passports Kit's entitled to is an American one; there is the street-wise demotic in which

Kit's negotiations with the fishing village's floating summer population of draft-dodgers, dope-pushers, and the unhappily self-exiled, are conducted. Even the village itself and its native inhabitants seem to share Kit's unstable relation to place and culture. Iticino is a place which, like Kit, has already known many identities. Originally a Greek settlement and then a Roman one, conquered by the Saracens and then the Spanish, it is now Italian (or is it Sicilian . . .?). Tourists are the most recent physical invaders, Hollywood the most recent cultural one: the younger fishermen communicate with tourists in 'an English backed by gestures learned from the movies as expected of them.'

Just as language – of voice and body – is unfixed, so too is Kit's sense of identity. After three weeks of an earlier brief and unsuccessful foray into boarding-school life in Switzerland, Kit had found that 'I hardly recognized myself, I affected a more precise English accent as my distinguishing mark and an avid and quirky taste for scholarship that couldn't be satisfied by any of the staff. In fact I wore myself as a mask, which is why I no longer have a self.'

It is also, perhaps, why Kit has difficulty in perceiving clearly and understanding those other selves who give life most meaning – Kit's parents and, more recently, Ajax, initially father's newest secretary, now also mother's much adoring, much adored lover.

For Kit, love has long been a problem. Well versed to the point of *ennui* in sexual passion as it is depicted in the world's legends, myths, art and philosophy, the child narrator is in reality utterly ignorant of its force and meaning, and is certainly wretchedly unprepared for the power of filial jealousy unleashed when an adored mother takes a lover. Kit is indeed thoroughly unconvinced of the very existence of love, outside the world of Art and Myth:

> How had artists invented the figment love I wondered. There was sex; mutual interest, companionship, affection even, but the grand passion that would tear the world to tatters didn't exist, even though literature, painting and music constantly celebrated it.

So *how* – but not, apparently, why – had artists invented the figment love? That is the question which exercises Kit who seeks the answer throughout a long, turbulent family summer holiday spent somewhere on the Mediterranean coast.

Not to know is always a torment for Kit. ('How could I have been so contemptibly innocent?', is the child's angry response to an earlier failure of knowledge.) Knowledge brings security for a child growing up within this daunting family. Kit races towards an adult sophistication in a desperate effort to bridge the otherwise terrifying gulf between child and parents:

> In our family ignorance and stupidity were held if not as crimes certainly as defects. My parents had compassion for the invincibly cretinous but they also had nothing to say to

them . . . . It was a constant terror to me that I might find myself on the other side, among the unwashed barbarian horde, and see them turn away.

Knowledge also brings enhanced status amongst contemporaries, and with those older in years, lesser in learning, though not, perhaps, in experience. As Jude, an almost-friend from the days in Switzerland, says, in words which hindsight endows with prescience: 'You think you know it all but all you know is from books. You walk about so superior kidding them all, despising everyone else, but I know you through and through.' Jude's claim to know fills Kit with terror: '"You can't", I said. "No one can know that!" But I was afraid.'

Kit is afraid because knowledge, as Kit well knows, is also power – and the power that knowledge confers, with its benign uses and malign perversions, is a major theme of this book. There is the power that Kit's internationally renowned, economist father wields over states and governments. There is the power that a medico-magical knowledge of herbs and drugs gives Signora Gambardella, the Iticino housekeeper and local witch. Most significant of all, there is the power that Kit so guilefully and insistently seeks throughout *Love Child*: the power that comes to the one who jealously watches lovers, who pinpoints the start and growth of love, charts and predicts its course, seeks to dictate its end. To possess knowledge is, or so Kit assumes, to possess the thing or person known. Possession's several meanings – a thing owned; the act of sexual 'taking'; a heightened emotional state, induced by divine or diabolical intervention – constantly collide, fuse and break apart again in *Love Child*.

Security, status, power: all these things knowledge can confer. In the wrong hands, it also brings danger. And Kit's hands, we soon learn, are supremely dangerous, for where sexual love is concerned, Kit is 'knowing' rather than knowledgeable, knows 'about' things, rather than knowing things, or people, themselves. The child is dauntingly clever, formidably articulate, intellectually sophisticated, shrewdly observant, skilfully manipulative and well informed about the mechanics of sexual activity. But intellectual development has to a grotesque extent outstripped emotional growth. As no less an authority than Kit repeatedly tells us, Kit is 'a monster'; and, as so often in this book, Duffy holds the two meanings of a word in perfect tension: Kit proves 'monstrous' in the colloquial sense of someone inhuman, capable of terrible deeds, but the child is also 'a monster' in that earlier, more aweful sense, of being a prodigy – a creature so rare as to appear outside and beyond nature.

Words such as 'monster' and 'prodigy' take us into the world of myth and fable, and it is in the language of myth and legend, fable and faery tale, and with constant allusions to their stories, that much of Kit's narrative is told. That well stuffed head is full of the myths of ancient Greece and Rome, is thoroughly familiar with the uses to which Renaissance poets and painters put them, is effortlessly able to draw analogies between the Ajax of today and Adonis, Actaeon and Icarus of the ancient world; to make comparisons between Kit's modern mother and Venus, Diana or Cleopatra. There's even a part built in for Kit – as Cupid, Venus's troublesome offspring, the child of Love, a Love child who has little of childhood's supposed innocence, little even of its youth. As Gerry, a young American woman passing through Iticino for the summer, tells Kit: 'Sometimes you seem to me like some spiteful elderly cupid played by a dwarf instead of a child' (and immediately the mind's eye conjures up one of those sinister, bald homunculi who scuttle and scamper into the corners of Beardsley's drawings). As the affair between Kit's mother and Ajax progresses, Kit's conduct most closely resembles that of a cupid turned incurably malign, who hovers, leers, spies, tricks and cheats as diligently as any of the maverick *putti* who people the Renaissance canvases alluded to throughout the novel, and who adorn the cover of this book.

Yet although Kit draws so constantly on myths, this precocious child narrator fails to understand one of the most important things about them, which is that however fabulous their stories, however 'impossible' their magical and miraculous events, they are *true* in a sense that stretches beyond, and renders irrelevant, scientific or empirical truth. Kit makes the fundamental error of assuming that before a thing can be true it must be 'real'; by consigning love to the world of 'unreal' myth, Kit loses all possibility of finding an answer to that initial urgent question: How – and why – had artists invented the figment love? Instead, the worldly and sophisticated Kit can manage only a crude formulation in which exasperation masks an anxious and resentful bewilderment: 'They had kidded themselves they were in love. But it didn't exist, that state. It was for myth and fairy tale, to give people something to dream about and to explain things for psychiatrists.' Obstinately, the far less clever, but very much wiser, Gerry, insists, 'No, there's something else. I know.'

This is a book crammed with myths – from Greece and Rome; from Asia and Egypt; from the Old and New Testaments; from Shakespeare and Proust; from Hollywood and 'B' films. What many of them have in common is metamorphosis – that moment of transition from one being to another, from one state to another: Zeus turning himself into a cloud, the better to engulf and possess one of his more unwilling mortal loves; or the pagan goddess of Love resurfacing as St. Venus, a Christian saint worshipped in Mediterranean coastal towns, including Iticino. (It's no coincidence that, early in the book, Kit's mother uses the time spent waiting for Kit in a child psychologist's office not to riffle through *Vogue* or *Harper's and Queen*, but to read Ovid's *Metamorphoses*, that inexhaustible treasure house of magic and marvels upon which the West has drawn for almost two thousand years.)

Just as myths so often involve lovers metamorphosing and transforming themselves, the better to pursue or elude love, so too love itself is a transformer: outside the shape-shifting world of myth, however, it frequently works its transformations invisibly, in ways imperceptible to an observer, even one so driven as Kit. It is an inner landscape – of desire fulfilled, need met, worlds shared – that is transformed. 'We have fallen in love; our imaginations have entangled', says Kit's mother to Ajax, describing the mysterious fusion of two inner worlds often deemed inviolably separate.

Not surprisingly, Kit doesn't – can't – see it. Kit has already undertaken one metamorphosis: from child to monster. One more major transformation awaits: from a monstrous ignorance of love to the terrible knowledge with which the book ends. The time between Kit fills with a series of counterfeit transformations – masks, disguises, camouflages – assumed to dupe and, ultimately, endanger the adults who have so treacherously betrayed the angry child by moving into a realm whose existence must be denied by Kit because it cannot yet be understood.

Just as Kit seeks knowledge which, almost to the very end, proves elusive, so too Duffy denies readers of *Love Child* two pieces of information usually felt to be indispensable in the telling of a story of sexual love and jealousy. We never learn the gender of Ajax nor (although discussions of this novel constantly assume that Kit is female) do we learn that of the child narrator. Any description, simile or image which seems to indicate one sex is quickly followed by another which confounds the assumption. The technical challenge posed by the decision is considerable – how do you write without pronouns? – and it is one which Duffy has embraced in other, later novels, notably *Londoners* (1983). It is equally challenging to the reader, forced to consider the part gender plays in shaping both the story (any story) and the reader's response to it. Is Kit a boy or a girl, jealous of a man or woman? At one level the uncertainty focusses attention purely on the emotions themselves; at another it keeps the reader in a state of perpetual disorientation, confronting the supreme importance and irrelevance of gender. In a reader's mind Ajax and Kit may undergo constant metamorphoses, moving between male and female as the reader's needs or preferences, assumptions or doubts dictate.

Love Child is not a book to be read quickly or skimmed. Duffy has always been as much a poet as a novelist and her prose in this novel is as densely textured as poetry, shot full of echoes, word-play and allusions. The novel explores and extends some of the preoccupations and themes already voiced in *Lyrics for the Doghour*, a collection of poetry which Duffy published in 1968. Poems such as 'The Letter', which begins 'Times I am a child shut out / From the converse of adults', remind us that part of ourselves may remain eternal child, eternal Kit. Poems structured upon images of the lover as hunter, the beloved as quarry, echo *Love Child*'s constant awareness that fierce urgency and 'a rage for possession' is as much a part of sexual love as gentleness and mutuality. This is something Duffy has always continued to assert: it, together with her unabashed championing of the butch, has led frequently in the past to attacks upon her work for its 'male-identified' protagonists and for its politically 'suspect' insistence that, pure or not, sexual desire is inextricably entangled with feelings which draw upon the emotional vocabulary of conquest and possession.

Lyrics for the Doghour also returns constantly to the relations between love, art, inspiration and death. One poem ('Number XXII' in the title-sequence), in which a lover finds her beloved figured everywhere in a gallery of pictures, takes us particularly close to *Love Child*'s central issues. The poem begins,

And fondly expecting to find you everywhere
The pictures are full of you,

and goes on to describe how each painting evokes 'every tone and tint of you', so that

The miles of painted women
Are you galleried,

and . . . you are hung
In every apse and alcove of my thought.

Here the tidy boundaries between the woman who inspires art and the art she inspires dissolve: she becomes a work of art in herself. 'My mother is a work of art', says Kit early in the novel. Yet even though Ajax may find Kit's mother hangs in every apse and alcove of her lover's thought, Ajax also knows that 'A person may be like a work of art which even if you hang on your wall you don't possess.' 'That,' says Kit's mother 'would be a very rare person.' 'Yes, most rare', replies Ajax, held in that moment which possibly marked the beginning of love.

The great themes of *Love Child* – the use and abuse of knowledge, the truthfulness of myth, the potent links between love and death, the power of art to hold mortality at bay – had then, already been identified in

Duffy's earlier writings and have continued to inform her work. In *Love Child* though, they attain peculiarly perfect expression. The prose is often richly sensuous in content, invariably stripped and pared in style. Punctuation within a sentence is used only if lack of it would make meaning genuinely unclear. So perfectly are sentences constructed that there is never any risk of confusion; but, accustomed as we have become to punctuation used often merely to mark a pause for breath, Duffy's sparing use of it forces us to pay proper attention to the way thought unfolds in her sentences.

Love Child can never be a lazy read, although it is an intensely pleasurable one. Five times over the past fifteen years I have tried to bring this book back into print. I am delighted that with its inclusion in the Lesbian Landmark series, new readers at last have the opportunity to discover a book which I believe to be one of the tiny handful of truly outstanding modern novels.

Alison Hennegan, Cambridge 1993

Part One

"If heaven would make me such
another world
Of one entire and perfect chrysolite,
I'd not have sold her for it."

Othello
William Shakespeare

It was i who christened my mother's lover. You notice that I say "I" rather than "me." I am a precocious child and my precocity has reached that formal phase where it is better to be right than liked. I say "christened" too, I suppose, shying away from "baptized" because of that other baptism and yet to give a more ritual flavour to the act than merely "named": the labelling of an object as Adam did with the animals though it is true my mother's lover was perhaps more animal than the rest of us and certainly our object.

"My mother's lover" is of course hindsight. They weren't lovers then and I shall come to that in time; possibly not the proper time as narratives should proceed but I know all about that and how as artist I can shape time to my fancy. I have read enough of Proust for my purposes and probably for my downfall. I have the tyranny of a child still, which I invoke to tell you how and when I will, savouring for my pleasure and meandering as I wish, as if I had gone fishing on a hot afternoon under a heavy cloak of dark oak and maple and been drawn deep into pools and flashed and skittered among pebbles in the wake of a spiny sunfish or dazed with heat and dazzle fallen into a mating dream of black damsel flies, following the saraband of their elegant soixante-neuf from flat rock bed to sedge hammock, and waking on the hard bank prickled with sweat and the warm dank air had tried to piece it all out for you.

But there must be a beginning. So I came into the drawing room of our London home where the light falls chastened by a tall, and venerated because venerable, acacia through the long stone-framed windows and the corners are populous with shadows and my father was saying, "What shall we call you then if you don't like your own name? Kit, this is my new secretary."

I was aware of my mother suddenly stepping forward in the dim angle of the room furthest from the day and back again like a nervous thoroughbred or the small hound the English call a whippet, an exposed quivering nerve of a dog with a translucent skin and the terrified shut sea-anemone eyes of a Velázquez lap spaniel. My mother's lover stood and smiled in the only patch of sunlight on the violet carpet. "Ajax," I said.

My father frowned. "It's the name for a dog or someone more brawn than brains. Besides he came to a bad end."

"I meant Ajax the lesser," I said. "And anyhow don't you expect faithful service?" I was less subtle in those days and I wanted to defeat him with my greater knowledge.

"He came to a bad end too," said my mother from her shade. "He was drowned for impiety." I could never defeat her.

"Ajax will do very well," and my mother's lover laughed.

My father frowned again. I wonder now if even then he felt he had made a mistake. His personal secretaries, boys and girls, are chosen for their beauty as much as anything else. It is understood that the duties will be fluid and the salary, or should one call it wage, excellent. If it isn't understood on engagement it becomes so, like a sugar lump taking up hot coffee, drawing it through itself until it melts into the fierce liquid though only held with one white facet against the scalding surface. My father is hot and strong and all pervading. He consumes them. His immortality is nourished on their youth as the gods bit into Iduna's golden apples. They never complain. Perhaps he pays them too well. Only twice has there been any trouble. Tino wished to stay in America when his time was up. His ticket was bought. He tried blackmail. He knew the laws of Massachusetts (we had spent the spring at the farm while my father was preparing a lecture course for Tokyo). He was summoned home by a letter from his mother. Then in Tokyo (that was a bad year) flaxen Inge wept that she was pregnant. It was not, of course, my father's child. She was well provided for. My father is diplomat as well as economist. He must judge, forecast, balance. That is his job and his talent. This is what the governments of the world, the financiers, the controllers of international organizations have employed and gilded him for over the years. Why did he fail so with Ajax? Is it the onset of age, the crumbling of him?

For it was his failure that brought Ajax among us. Whether it was observation or reason that told me as I looked at my mother's lover laughing in that glowing violet pool as if spotlit, a Japanese waterflower suddenly opened out of nothing in a glass, with a dapple of light-green motes flung across the white suit by a flickering of the acacia leaves, I can't say any more, too much having stepped between, but certainly Ajax was different from the others, older, more intelligent I realized, not abashed by my father. What had gone wrong?

As a rule he picked them up without difficulty. Asked to lunch at a college, to a reception, holding court at a party, he drew them to him, a Mesmer who had only to look into their eyes and speak from the grave depths of his authority and they would give up their lives to serve him for the few months it took to leech them pale. Had Tino and Inge shaken him?

"Why does Ajax want this job?" I asked my mother later.

"To travel I think. We're going to Iticino. Why do you ask?"

"Ajax is different." I lifted a corner of the Venetians and watched a blunt black cab beetle across the square.

"It's too soon to take against someone."

"On the contrary, I take for; oh very much so. It will be interesting to watch."

We are international. We do not belong to any one place or sometimes I think even to any one time. Where we were born is irrelevant. The plane touches down at some complex of spun concrete and glass whose all roads lead to the stars, our mother is whisked into the nearest whitely hushed clinic or nursing home and we are brought painlessly forth. I was born in Lausanne.

We are polyglot, polygamous, polymorphous, and polysyllabic. Between us we compass seven dead languages: my father from his student days at Uppsala has Norse and Anglo-Saxon, my mother from hers Greek,

Latin and Hebrew, while I have added Gaelic and she Sanskrit; and five living, apart from ubiquitous English and smatterings of Cantonese, Urdu, and Yoruba picked up on my father's travels. Foreign doesn't exist for us as a concept.

Everyone I know has been married several times except my mother. Everyone I know is a shapechanger while remaining of the same essence. No one says yes or no. Monosyllables are unamusing and undeniable.

I am terrified of us. We don't exist as other people exist, defined by their time and place and upbringing. We are the characters in fairy tales: Once upon a time (which time?) in a certain country (what country?) there lived a rich man and his wife (or king and queen?) and they had one . . . You read about us in the newspapers of the polyglot world; we look out at you from the aquarium screen. And I exist less than any of them for I am both too young and too old. Eventually I shall go to university somewhere, perhaps New York, and some identity may settle upon me or I shall be able to patch one together from a range of colourful eccentricities; before when I was a small child I was able to persuade others that I existed by the wilfulness and vehemence of my behaviour, able almost to persuade myself that if I shouted loud enough I might hear myself saying something. Then one day I listened, I couldn't help it, and there was nothing except noise. Now I am pupating. Touch my polished plastic shell and I may twitch my abdomen. If you can bring yourself to touch me. I am the chrysalis; my mother is the chrysolite.

I can't look beyond that. Beyond that will be work

and sex, both traditionally requesting some form of involvement if I live that long; if we live that long. Of course I could go now, to university I mean. I have the grades. With a list of set books I could take finals in a few months because I remember everything I read; its place on the page and in the book. But I am too young. My parents have bred a monster like the wizened child-Christ of Byzantine painting. I know everything but I am no more than a computer subtly programmed. *Cogito ergo non sum.*

Not that I believe, believed, in a heart or to be more precise in the opposition of intellect and emotion with virtue on the side of the natural feeling Man. I had simply always taken it for granted that everyone I knew was and had been the same, apart from a sharp attack of Romantic agony, emotional colic induced by repression, too-tight lacing in the nineteenth century, that calm and reason prevailed in private life not out of any deep conviction that it should be so but because no one, whatever temporary postures they might adopt, felt strongly enough for it to be otherwise. "Men have died and worms have eaten them but not for love." It's true there was Catullus, who would seem by all accounts to have pined to death like a dog for love of Lesbia. But statistically, as my father says, he wouldn't even equal a half unit, on any conceivable chart he wouldn't even rate putting in a decimal point. The numerous divorces in our circle weren't for passion but because the original couple had tired of living together; a new partner for either one was simply brought in as a convenient blanket to separate under, to give nausea an acceptable exit.

My mother had married young, my father before. I have grown half siblings with whom one exotic night I might commit putative incest. It's amazing how easily the taboos don't apply. Once Roddy stayed with us on his way to Perugia for a summer semester. That was very near except I was too young and knew no better than to take him fishing, wading far out so that my wet levis would cling close to me. But his mind had already gone ahead and he was only humouring me. I don't know at what point they came to their arrangement. Some time after I was born I imagine. He had his secretaries and she discreet and occasional one-night stands. My mother is beautiful and brilliant: she has only to want.

My mother is ugly. I have spoiled her. All children despoil their mothers in birth. They take from them unstretched muscles, unthickened nipples clung to only by lovers, not the tyrannous prehensile lips of infants; they stiffen and solidify. I shall never see her as a girl before my gravity set in, crescent, freeriding. Now she pivots about me in dutiful orbit.

It was the talk among the other children at school that taught me about my parents. I would have found out eventually anyway but my charming playfellows' chatter about their own ménages thrust the consideration of mine into my consciousness with the irresistibleness, the half-welcome violence of rape. Their tales flung me on my back and swept through me so that I had to clench my teeth not to cry out with the new knowledge so bitterly exciting and when I staggered up I was dazed and drenched and drew the threads of reason quickly about me as covering for the shame of my ignorance. It was not having realized that bruised. How could I have been so contemptibly innocent?

"It's time you went to school for a while," my father announced over his supervitaminised cereal one morning. Since I was six and my table manners sufficiently civilized I had eaten with them except when they gave a dinner party.

"Why?" I said. My mother had buried herself and her hardboiled egg behind a pile of mail which she was opening, holding each letter up high to read, but I felt her disapproval seep round the edges of her page. They were not united: it was worthwhile resisting.

"We are going to São Paulo and then Cuba. It's not a suitable place for you and it'll be too hot."

"I could stay here with Fantah." Fantah had looked after me since I was born. "Or go to Grand'mère." My father's mother was always delighted to see me. She would show me the Northern lights and I would sit warm inside her window and watch the snow piling among the shopping crowds in the sharp, soon-winter dark and the street lamps hung like baubles against the mica-black sky while other children shouted by on their small sleds. She would let me read until my eyes watered.

"You have to learn to deal with other people," my father said, "and to do that you must mix with them. You must go to school." Then I knew that I was beaten. On a liberal principle he is inflexible. My mother turned a page a little too clumsily and I knew she didn't agree. This was the moment when I first realized she loved me. She didn't want me to go away. Until then, like a child or animal, I had taken it for granted; now I realized it consciously and with that came the possibility of doubt.

My school had of course already been chosen, also on the most liberal principles: coeducational, free discipline, the Gambit system of individual development invented or devised by the principal, Dr. Gambit, so the brochure said. Money could buy no more. In addition there was skiing in the nearby Alpine foothills for winter, swimming in the school's own bit of lake, and pony trekking through the pine forests for summer. It had testimonials from half a dozen parents of international standing and proportionate fees. They saw me off at Heathrow one London spring morning. There was no such thing as an academic year at St. Gelbert. The florets of the acacia filled the drawing room with a fragile white fragrance that seemed to me a distillation of my mother's own perfume and for once funereal.

I look back now on myself sitting in my window seat behind the blade of wing as medieval man must have looked back to our pre-Fall parents. I was used to travelling alone. The stewardess was solicitous and I knew that my mother would have had a discreet word, perhaps sent one of her specially printed lilac cards in advance of me. At Geneva I was met by a smiling and perfect secretary in blue linen suit and white blouse who expertly guided us to the St. Gelbert train. For a while we traced the shore of the lake until we reached Lausanne, where I stared out at the station which might have been a clinic. "I was born here," I said.

"Were you? It's a very handsome town." The accent

was colonial English; I guessed South African.

"I've never been here since. It means nothing to me or at least that's not quite accurate: its meaning for me is a heavily underscored lack of meaning."

She smiled a little uncertainly and I turned to look back through the window, which was now rushing through a climbing and darkening mountainscape. I pictured the jointed pantograph pressed like the antennae of a steel bug against the flung loop of cable, dashing sparks along the valleys, the articulated segments gobbling up the track like a mammoth centipede and remembered a story of my father's about the first time Indians ever saw a train and how they thought it was a fire-breathing serpent that had swallowed the men in its belly. Gradually it slowed and laboured against steeper gradients. "We're almost there." She began to tug at the suitcases.

Outside the small station in the sharp air that clawed suddenly at the nostrils a dark blue Mercedes was waiting, chosen perhaps to suit her clothes, and she drove us to the school with the now familiar smiling efficiency. "This is your study. I expect you'd like to unpack." In the brochure it had said separate rooms and I had thought that at least I should be able to get away. There were necessary sparely modern furnishings; the central heating was adequate. I began to unpack.

"Hi!" A voice swung me round. Two children a little older than myself had come silently into the room in sneakers. The boy put out a hand first. "I'm Hollow." At least I thought that was what he had said.

"I'm Jude," the girl followed.

"Kit."

"It's really French time until after supper but we've been allowed to speak English because you're new. The Sex sent us along. You want a drag?" He extended a packet of Gauloises. Jude took one and flicked open a lighter.

"If you've got anything like this keep it on you. Things vanish fast around here. Now what can we tell you?"

"Almost anything. What's it like?"

"As foul as most but they ride you pretty easy. They slung half a dozen out last term for shoplifting in the village but that was a crazy thing to have done. Long as you're not a chunkhead you're alright."

"Yeah, you can be as weird as you like."

"You don't look like a chunkhead," Jude tapped her cigarette expertly.

"Just don't get the place in bad with the local gendarmes—that's the main thing. Gambit's terrified of closure. He'd sell you himself first."

"After all we're a pretty wild crew but as long as we keep it on the premises he doesn't care."

"Where've you been before?" Hollow asked the question I'd been dreading.

"Oh just around. Right now I've come from London. My parents are going to Cuba."

"Most of us have been chucked out of every school on the planet. My last one just folded under me," Jude said. "It was very exotic, all girls like camellias, and very sophisticated. The headmistress or should I say principal . . . ?" She rolled her eyes up until the whites showed. I noticed she carried a sheath knife in her belt like a scout.

"I'm head of the school council," Hollow said. "We run things ourselves."

"What does it mean, 'Hollow'?" I asked.

"Short for Holofurnace. Get it? When Jude told me what her name was I knew we had to be *copains* or she'd eat me up. We run things between us. You'd better tell Kit who to look out for." He nodded at Jude.

"Well there's Von Vörst. He thinks he's the last of the true Prussians. His father's a West German industrialist, a bit shady and very flash. Vörst despises him and practises the virtues of the old régime; keeps a machine gun under his bed. Then there's Staboul. His father's one of these little Arab princelings with an oildom. He's terrified of assassination so he shoots first and asks after."

"Yeah and watch out for Dara: she's always claiming she's been raped."

"They had to get rid of matron's dog because Dara swore it assaulted her. She's a whore. Then there's Anne Louise, whose old man's so loaded she worries all the time about kidnapping. She's sweet but very nervy."

A gong sounded below in the house. Hollow levered himself up from my bed. "I have to go see there's no trouble."

"I'm not hungry tonight," I said.

"See you then," he drifted out of the door, thumbs in the top of his belt.

"What's his problem?"

"Nothing. They all go up in smoke. Most of the time he's a little high. Watch his eyes."

"And you?"

She laughed and drew the knife out of its sheath.

Holding it flat against her palm she pointed it at me. "You're pretty. I like you." Then she threw it hard so that it struck quivering in the pine doorjamb, bent and retrieved it in one movement, and stuck it back in her belt.

The timetable was a model of simplicity. In the mornings there were seminars in all the traditional subjects for those who wanted to attend; in the afternoons the winter or summer sports of the prospectus. In three weeks I hardly recognized myself. I affected a more precise English accent as my distinguishing mark and an avid and quirky taste for scholarship that couldn't be satisfied by any of the staff. In fact I wore myself as a mask, which is why I no longer have a self. I refused to show an interest in any of the leisure activities. Games were for the young and immature intellects: I was suddenly very old.

"You're a weirdo and a whiz kid," Hollow complimented in his jargon of clichés. "You could make a fortune of your own."

"Money! I'm not for public exhibition."

Hollow was thin with great joints like an arthritic. When he banged the gavel at meetings his hands were big and raw like those of a Texan cattle auctioneer who had perhaps been one of his ancestors. He ruled because when he was high he would slalom down the most dangerous slopes as if the solid trees were ghostmist or snow and would melt at his touch. It was legend that he had once fallen, pierced a lung with a broken rib and gotten up and completed the run spitting red berries of blood into the white snow.

He sat on the edge of the platform in the assembly hall, his long legs dangling, insect or puppet, the rest lounging or squatting is an aggressive unkemptness of dress and posture. I stood at the back, arms folded across my chest with conscious calm; Jude leaned against the platform like Hollow's bodyguard, her pelvis thrust forward, the knife threateningly quiet against her thigh.

"We've got to clean this place up," Hollow began in best gangster idiom. "For most of us there's no place else we can go and it's up to us to keep this afloat. That means we've got to apply a bit of discipline to ourselves and I think we start with a handing in of offensive weapons."

"What happens to them?" demanded an urchin whose mother was a singer who found his presence and age so embarrassing he had stunted his own growth. Indeed, looking about, I felt myself a kind of Peer Gynt in the hall of the mountain king, though perhaps at that moment I seemed very little different from the others and each of them had separated himself in his own mind in the same way.

"We lock them in a closet."

"Who shall keep the key?" asked Anne Louise, "to have access to all those weapons!"

"I shall," said Hollow.

"And why should we trust you?" Staboul demanded and Von Vörst growled his assent. For once they were united.

"Because I'm a pacifist. I don't need your guns, man."

"You are a decadent," Von Vörst said. He was a thin rigid boy, his cropped hair dabbed with peroxide to keep it Aryan blond. Staboul wore a sheepskin surcoat, headcloth, and gold twined band as well as pants and shirt.

"This is a democracy," Hollow said. "We shall vote

on it." All hands were raised for him except Staboul's and Von Vörst's. "Majority decision."

"I will give mine up if he will give his," Staboul jerked his head at the Prussian. "I do not trust him."

"Why should I abide by the collective will of ignorant and effete children? The mass is to be led, not to govern."

"Because we shall make you," said Hollow. "You will stay here while Jude and Kit collect your armoury."

Von Vörst scowled and looked around for escape but we were already slipping out of the door while the others stood about him, Lilliputians enough to bring down a Gulliver. I saw his mind baulk at the indignity.

We found the gun easily, its shape unmistakeable through the protective wrapping of sheet. Jude unwound its shroud and exposed the dead and gleaming thing that was as beautiful as polished bones, coolly complacent in its self-existence. It didn't need human agency to set it in motion or at least so it seemed. At any moment it might spit death of its own will. We had conceived it and yet it had more sense of separateness, that entity that artifacts possess in their three dimensionalness, than its breathing warm creators, with their constant demands to sustain life, their mutual dependence, their to and flow of needs. Jude let the sheet drop like an unveiling ceremony and sidled her finger onto the button.

"Careful!" I knew that she would point it at me.

"Chicken; it's not loaded. We've got to find the clips too."

"Why? They're no good without the tool." I picked the word carefully out of my arsenal.

"He might break them open, make a little heap of gunpowder and whoof!"

"Molotov cocktails."

"You don't need powder for them."

"It's the principle not the recipe I mean."

"Look under his bed again," she motioned at me with the short barrel.

I got down on hands and knees. The reek of Von Vörst's bedding fell on me thickly, stiflingly. He slept between blankets, sheets were effeminate. I thought of his bony limbs caught in the rough male kiss and wondered if he masturbated or if he believed it might spoil his manhood. Suddenly I felt something hard pressing into the crease between my buttocks. I knew what it was at once, had unconsciously expected it.

"Hurry up," Jude said.

"How can I look with you shoving that thing up my arse?" Once again I picked the words carefully, let them fall coldly to keep myself equal and stifle panic. She laughed but moved the muzzle away. "There they are." I lay flat on my belly and wormed my way farther under the bed, stretching out a hand to the cardboard carton against the wall. I pulled it towards me and rolled out, panting and red-faced. It was full of magazine clips. Together we proceeded back to the hall, Jude behind like my jailer. I set the box down on the platform.

"Scum," said Von Vörst, "you run together like the jackals you are, Jews and blacks and half breeds, but one day we who work in secret and alone will destroy you even if we must destroy this whole planet with you and begin again elsewhere with only the pure and the strong."

"I hope you've got your rocket ready, Father Noah," Hollow said. "Lock 'em up."

"They are my property but I do not expect you to have respect for such a concept."

"You can have them back when you leave," said Hollow. "Now yours," he nodded at Staboul, who took his pistol from his holster and gave it to him butt first. "And those," he indicated the crossed bandoliers ribbed with bullets. Staboul unslung them, leaving deep caterpillar tracks in the dirty snow of his skeepskin. "And the rest of you." One after the other they came up like the saved at an evangelist's meeting and dropped their armoury in a heap beside the closet, slings, knuckledusters, the baseball bat used as cosh, the goblin's iron-shod lance made from a broken ski stick.

"What about hers?" asked Staboul.

"Jude?"

Reluctantly the knife was unsheathed and added. She looked somehow smaller without it. "And hers," Jude said.

"Come on, Dara," Hollow's voice was firm.

"I'm afraid." She was visibly shaking.

"We'll look after you," Hollow held out his hand and eventually she drew a wicked steel pin from her belt.

Carefully we loaded them all in the closet. Hollow ceremonially locked the door and threading a sneaker lace through the key slung it around his neck.

As I lay in my bed that night, a hand inside my pyjama pants gently caressing myself, I thought of the locked closet and Von Vörst creeping down in the dark to reclaim his weapon, and then I knew that he wouldn't, that the ritual would bind him as it would the rest but that now they would have to find other masks to protect themselves, the assumed shells and overgrown snappers that concealed the soft abdomen. There is a small lovely crustacean called a hermit crab that squats its vulnerable belly in the discarded fortresses of other shellfish. Comes the time when its home pinches like an outgrown shoe, it begins to belch from its cramped gut, it gasps, its eyes pop and pincers turn numb and blue. It must move, must drag its backside out of its tenement and across the abrasive ocean bed to a new roomier retreat while the terrors hover ready to pounce and devour it. This is the terrifying moment repeated periodically throughout its life until one day it's too big and too slow. Such a moment was being enacted all over the building. I wondered if one of the staff going the rounds, pausing outside each door, was aware of the groans, the rustlings as the lonely vulnerable children shot themselves off for comfort in the dark. For the next few days they would be more aggressive, sharper as they tussled for new defences against each other and themselves. My hand moved faster until in a minute I too was shuddering and jerking into sleep.

In the morning I slept late, missing the communal piggery of breakfast, the tables confettied with cornflakes and sugar, puddled with milk, the smell of frowsty children tumbled from bed, the obscenity of fried eggs, their yellow pupils under a filmy cataract of grease set in ragged whites. I took myself to a literature seminar intended for those taking English qualifying examinations though I was too young to sit the test itself. The prescribed book was Shakespeare's *Othello*, which I knew from both the opera my parents had taken me to in Milan and the play done in a student production on a remote campus my father was speaking at on the underdeveloped countries: The Barren Fig Tree—Utilizing Our Wastes.

"Already we have the concept of the passionate Negro, a simple man whose feelings are more violent than those of the more sophisticated Venetians which is why he is such a good general but also an easy instrument for Iago to play on. His excessive jealousy is a primitive reaction resulting in a primitive solution: murder. This is not to suggest that Shakespeare was a racist, only that he was able to use conventional ideas of his time, and ours, and make great drama out of them."

"Was Leontes black?"

"I'm sorry Kit, I don't quite . . . ?"

"I was just thinking that Leontes has less motive than Othello, no Iago to prompt him, yet his actions and reactions are even more violent and irrational."

"Quite so. What we should perhaps be considering is Iago's motive."

"Surely his motives are all rationalizations to cover his inverted sexual fear and hatred of Othello. Unless we consider Othello and Iago as two aspects of the one personality." I had heard my parents discussing this at breakfast.

"Yes, well that's certainly something to chew over before we meet again." The gong sounded his release.

In the afternoons the building was deserted, children and staff gone away to the cold snow slopes except for matron in her quarters next to the sick bay, so I was surprised to hear the foghorn of some low-voiced string instrument coming from Jude's study. I knocked.

"Who is it?"

"Kit." There was a pause.

"You can come in." I pushed open the door. "Now lock it. If you're wandering about others might be too."

"I didn't see anyone. In fact I didn't know you were here til I heard the cello. Even then, I mean I didn't know . . ."

"Nobody does. In a place like this they'd think you were soft if you let on to something as civilized as music."

I thought she was probably wrong but I didn't object. It seemed to me that St. Gelbert's would take anything as long as you put it over with sufficient panache; certainly no one had tried to edge under my own mask. Each was too busy inside himself. Maybe Jude needed to keep it secret.

"I'm going to get my knife back."

"How?"

"I got the key from Hollow when he was high."

"Won't he miss it?"

"I'll put it back next time he's on a trip. Tonight."

"You won't be able to wear it."

"No. But I don't want it in there jumbled up with all the rest. I need it."

"That's what they all think."

"When are your parents getting divorced?" She slapped the question across my face so that I blinked and almost stepped back.

"They're not."

"Of course they are. Why else would they send you here. You're being ditched like the rest of us while they split."

"My father's been divorced once."

"So. Hollow's got three daddies and two mommies."

"What about you?" I tried to turn the game.

"I'm a love child; my parents opted out of the whole mess."

"Then why're you here?"

"My mother was killed in a car crash. My father travels."

"I'm sorry."

"Be sorry for yourself. Cuba! Reno or Las Vegas."

"They never lie to me. If there was anything they'd say."

"All grownups lie. Watch them, listen for the pauses. They can't tell us because they've made the rules and they've broken them but no one must know and we have to be brought up to keep the rules too. What a mess! Why not just chuck it all away and start with something simple. You watch them, you listen. You'll soon see. Any day now you'll be called to old Gambit and with a mourning face he'll tell you the bad news."

"They'd tell me themselves."

"Not them. You wait. You'll find they're like all the rest."

"Why are you so bloody cruel?" It was a mistake but she'd hurt me.

"Because you're such a child. You think you know it all but all you know is from books. You walk about so superior kidding them all, despising everyone else but I know you through and through."

"You can't," I said. "No one can know that!" But I was afraid. Jude was overpowering. Her strength reached down into me and twisted a knot of terror out of my diaphragm.

"I bet you don't even masturbate."

I was glad she had used the technical term instead of St. Gelbert's jargon, which my four-week familiarity with the *phrases idiomatiques* might have been unequal to. "Of course I do. What do you think I am?"

"Let's see," and she took me by the belt of the levis that I had assumed like the rest as undress school uniform with ski pants for formal wear.

No one had ever touched me before yet I understood; I had read enough. Where her hands moved flames licked up so that I was powerless to pull away as she undid the zipper. "You're a virgin," she said. "You'll go like a bomb." I braced my leg muscles to keep me from falling and as the pain and pleasure bit through me I heard her say, "It isn't love, Kit, it isn't love." My mouth filled with ash.

There was a phone in the hall but I didn't use that. I walked to the village to the bar. *"Je veux téléphoner . . ."* The address seemed to surprise the operator, who told me rather suspiciously that I must book a call. I waited for an hour, drinking cup after cup of black coffee until my heart was pounding and my nerve ends twitched under the skin. *"C'est à moi!"* I called when the phone rang. The proprietor picked up and silently held the receiver out to me. Her voice sounded very far away. I learned later they weren't yet up. "You've got to come and get me."

"Why, Kit? What's the matter?"

"I'm not prepared to waste any more time here. I'd

learn more bumming round the world with a jellyroll."

"A what?"

"Never mind. Anyhow, I'm leaving this place."

"That's a kind of blackmail."

"I know." There was a pause. I tried hard to hear her breathing, to counter the mechanical silence.

"Is it that urgent?"

"Yes." Again a pause. Maybe they were conferring together.

"Your father has a bank account in Geneva."

"Yes."

"We'll contact them. Don't worry, darling. It won't be long. As short as I can make it. Now go back to school and be patient."

"You promise?"

"I promise."

I waited two days, locked in my room most of the time, going down to the village for food I sneaked in and ate alone. On the third day there was a knock on my door. "Who is it?"

"Dr. Gambit would like to see you," called the secretary's voice.

"I'll come at once." Jude's words in my head made me feel sick and weak but I got up from the bed where I'd been lying, combed my hair, and unlocked the door.

"It seems your parents can't get along without you," the headmaster said and gave me a letter. It was from my father's bank enclosing flight instructions and tickets. "You haven't much time to get your things together. Do you think you can be ready?"

"I think so." I tried not to seem too eager.

"Miss Sexton will drive you to the station." He held out his hand. "I'm sorry it's only been short, Kit. Good luck."

"Goodbye." I shook his hand. If I have ever had any attempt at a childhood it was over. I had listened to the conversations at table and among the lounging groups in the evening and had thought that what they said didn't apply to me, to us. Jude, although I had refuted her words so strongly, had made me doubt and her hands on my thighs had sown their tales, dragon's teeth deep in my gut. I saw them hatch like maggots in the intestine of a dead animal and consume my disbelief and my ignorance so that now, returning, I watched and listened so that I should never be caught naked again.

And now I understood it all: the sudden cessation of conversation when I came into the room, the mutual politeness, the trips never inquired about, the changing faces of our household, the unexplained tension from time to time. I didn't question. I didn't want either my suspicions confirmed or them to lie to me. I was too old for that. My only emotions were anger that my innocence had made me vulnerable and shame. You might argue that it's waste of emotional energy to be ashamed of a state that because of one's youth and upbringing one couldn't help but then one is ashamed of the acne of adolescence, the withered arm, one's inability to speak the language of the country one is visiting even if it's Pushtu. One is ashamed because one is in some way inadequate, imperfect measured by some ideal. In our family ignorance and stupidity were held if not crimes certainly as defects. My parents had compassion for the invincibly cretinous but they also

had nothing to say to them. My father shook their hands
and dropped platitudes on their heads; my mother backed
away into a shy tense silence unable to deal with either
them or her own guilt. Only beauty and reason could save
the world, and confronted by the enormity of what these
tender sidereal twins must conquer she withdrew into a
tenacious pessimism that knew we were doomed as Leo-
nidas and yet like him had no choice but to fight on. It was
a constant terror to me that I might find myself on the
other side, among the unwashed barbarian horde, and see
them turn away. Sometimes I heard my voice rushing into
opinions I felt they would find naïve and then I stuttered
and apologized. They were always patient and rational and
I need not have worried but I didn't know then that I was
a monster.

Perhaps my father had been right to insist on St. Gelbert's. Certainly in my four weeks there I learned the only
two things I would have taken much longer to find out, or
might never have realized, at home: the first Jude taught
me; the second Hollow helped me to.

My mother didn't question me on my return. I had
gone home to our Massachusetts farm and Fantah to
await their arrival and I tried to divert myself from my
new knowledge by going fishing, walking the long humid
track between the overtopping corn, where at night as I
lay awake I heard the farmers popping off at the lemur-
eyed raccoons which were every child's cuddly panda toy,
til my feet were caked with dust and sweat and I reached
my favourite bit of river with the stepping stones, where
I played at being a child while I waited to test my adult
wisdom.

"What was wrong with it?" my father asked.

"We did hardly any work and what we did was too easy." I felt him metaphorically raising an eyebrow at my mother.

"It could be true. Kit's used to working alone and we've no idea of the standard."

"I think a visit to an educationist. A few tests and we know where we are."

We took a plane to New York. "Are you nervous?" she asked.

"Not a bit. Nothing depends on it, does it?"

"No," she smiled. "Nothing at all."

"Then I'll enjoy it—like a quiz or a crossword."

"Good."

"You're a weirdo and a whiz kid," Hollow said in my head.

The lady in the capuccino-coloured dress with features made from a selection of fervid *petits fours* played games with me for an hour or so while my mother sank herself in Ovid's *Metamorphoses*, disdaining the pile of glossies on the gleaming table of the waiting room. Finally when I had read to the lady, identified shapes for her, written lists of opposites and families, told her stories from ink blots, matched figures, found odd men out until I felt like Kim training for The Great Game, and expected her to empty a box of assorted stones onto the pale blue table for my re-membrance (blue, I reflected at one point, because it was soothing and kindergarten and why didn't she shave the black wells of her armpits for the same reason?) my mother was called in while I took her place.

"Well," said my father, "how did you get on?"

"Did you know you have a photographic memory?" my mother asked.

"Yes," I said. "I always have had. Doesn't everyone?"

"No. The rest of us have to remember things the hard way."

"It's not much use without the ability to understand what you remember." My father sounded a bit huffed.

"I don't think we need worry about that with Kit's I.Q."

"And reading age?"

"Doesn't come into it," she said. "It's gone beyond measuring, off the page."

My father didn't know whether to be pleased or piqued. "Figures?"

"Needs a little coaching."

"No more schools," I put in quickly. "It's not worth it just for math. I shall run away."

"Blackmail, Kit," she said.

"I have to," I said. "Honestly, it's the only way."

"We'll talk it over." It was the signal to leave. I went out into the hall and let them hear my steps climbing the stairs then going into the bathroom, where, I knew from experience, it was possible to hear what was said in the aptly named parlour. I had worked out these acoustics when I was quite small and had been struck one day by how clearly one could hear the sounds of running water from below. It should work both ways. I also knew that four walls give people a sense of security of not being overheard. Unless one is used to the idea of surveillance, that the room is bugged, out of sight means not only out of mind but out of hearing.

"Our child is rather unusual," I heard my mother say.

"Perhaps a day school?"

"It would either mean constant changes or leaving Kit in one place while we're away."

"London would be better than here." I held my breath partly not to miss her answer, partly the better to will what she should say.

"I just can't see it. I don't think Kit's the type to rough it among a constant stream of strangers and with that degree of intelligence I don't feel we should risk it. There was a suggestion, though of course as an education-ist rather than a psychiatrist she didn't elaborate, that Kit might be a bit what used to be called 'sensitive.'"

"Surely that's old-fashioned."

"It's an oversimplification. Even so, I don't think it's a good idea for a child to be too much alone."

"You mean we must provide some society for our growing genius if it's not to have its little playfellows." I felt rather than heard her laugh. "What about the math? A child can't be innumerate if it's to live in the twenty-first century." My father was always aware of the future. Indeed he had a fantastic grasp of all time, which made him seem Jehovahesque; minutes and millennia were held in his mind not only precisely but imaginatively, so that listening to one of his lectures on say illiteracy among Rus-sian serfs of the eighteenth century was like reading Push-kin or a first-hand account.

"A tutor?"

"Nothing wrong with that. I'd do it myself except that I haven't the time and Kit's probably too old to learn from me any more." He had indeed taught me elementary arithmetic by playing card games, particularly cribbage, with me and Fantah. Then he had taught me decimals and fractions, so that I should understand something of statistics when they discussed them, and later percentages. Not needing to listen any further I flushed the john.

From that time I never left them. My tutors came and went even more regularly than my father's secretaries and after a couple of years ceased altogether, to be renewed at my discretion when I should be old enough for a university somewhere. Soon I was included in my parents' dinner and supper parties and applied my new knowledge to the people I met there, a constant procession for my study. The more I studied the more Jude's words seemed to me a just appraisal. How had artists invented the figment love I wondered. There was sex, mutual interest, companionship, affection even, but the grand passion that would tear the world to tatters didn't exist, even though literature, painting, and music constantly celebrated it. Perhaps it was a myth like God thought up to fill a need and to convince human beings that in prolonging the race they were part of something both magnificent and beautiful. I didn't question my parents about it because I didn't want them to know that I knew and also I was afraid that they too would find themselves unable to do without this offer of a personal Utopia and would either lie to me or let me see their inadequacy by pretending to themselves. I didn't want them dethroned yet. Then there would be nothing. Before St. Gelbert's I hadn't thought of love. My response to Roddy had been unreflecting and I can't now decide whether that afternoon by the river was a damsel fly flicker of that legendary emotion or just sex.

> "Young I am, and yet unskill'd
> How to make a lover yield;
> How to keep, or how to gain,
> When to love, and when to feign.
>
> Take me, take me some of you
> While I yet am young and true;"

The last time I could have claimed company with Dryden's virgin I was too young to be worth the taking. Jude, supplying some strange need of her own, made thinking and rejecting the same act as if as she had touched me into automatic ecstasy she dropped an ice splinter into my heart from the flawed frozen crystal of her own and ruptured my emotional virginity as though it had never been. To keep it after the age of puberty is to go through life in a caul; to have mislaid it so young seems closer to perversity than to mere youthful carelessness. Yet at the time I was angry with myself ever to have suffered it.

I appraised my father's choices with an amused and dispassionate eye; my mother's were hidden from me, though once on a plane journey I thought I caught a look between her and a red-haired man that made the palms of my hands go numb with excitement while at the same time I was surprised and amused by the red hair and that she should respond to it.

And so, after this gentle-reader digression on my schooling to explain me and introduce us, much like Ibsen's despised first act, we return to Ajax. I have cautioned you to accept my seeming irrelevances which, like an old world charm, I stucco over my skeleton of precast concrete and milled steel. I am a gutted Nash terrace on which daily I perform a clinical and utilitarian conversion behind my classic preserved façade of a simple innocent human child.

My father had picked out (had it been anyone else I would have said picked up) Ajax at an obscure training college on the West coast of Wales. I've never been there but I can imagine it very well: wind-bitten mountains, black rocks, spray and drizzle and the sheep more amiable than the human cattle. He never refused a request to lecture anywhere, however remote in location or likely response. I can imagine too the sherry in the staff common room after, before the boiled institution lunch or dinner; my father's despair of finding anyone to talk to among the disguised clergy who staff such missionary outposts, carrying the gospel according to St. Job among the natives who might otherwise be bright and free, and renew his dynamic force, strength having gone out of him at the lecture, which he did always by earthing that of others in himself or by setting up a field of energy between the two poles in a dialogue to charge up his diminished battery. And Ajax would be drawn to my father by a similar impulse, perhaps after months of slow corrosion weakening the brain cells. There would be a flash in that dank twilight academy that my father would mistake for admiration and sex. Maybe the lights weren't too good either, causing him also to mistake the age of my mother's lover and let out the: "I don't know how you stand it here."

And the answer: "Neither do I."

"We must do something about it. How would you

feel . . . ?" And my mother's lover surprised at the warmth, the concern of the offer saying, "Yes. I could come at the beginning of the vacation," being both impulsive and an innocent.

I didn't of course in that first moment in the drawing room know all this; only vaguely I sensed that there was something not so much wrong as amiss. In the beginning they always looked at my father with an adoring puppy stare which, I've remarked, puppies never direct at the humans that supposedly own them but almost inwards as if towards their own small and enchanting selves (it was perhaps this well of appreciation that he drew upon). As they matured (and this came upon them as rapidly as puppies grow from week to week) they became aggressive and smouldering, their eyes flashy and sulky by turns but now fixed upon my father until at the last they were glazed and indifferent. Then they left. Ajax' eyes were cool; they smiled. Whatever lay behind them was not to be drawn up easily. Ajax looked out from behind glass.

"When do we go?" I said to my mother, dropping the corner of the blind on the scurrying beetle.

"On Thursday."

"And how do *you* take?"

"Like you, very much for."

I had risked a direct question, something we don't do in our family, and was surprised at the directness of the answer only slightly turned by the reference to my own words. I had wondered since coming back from school what she thought about my father's recurring secretaries, what arrangement they had come to between them. I realized suddenly that the reason I never asked her a direct question but always hid it behind some stylistic veil was that if so asked she would answer with the truth and her truth might terrify me.

We have, as well as the Massachusetts farm and the London flat, a villa in Iticino. There is also a châlet perched on the edge of the least tourist frequented Alp the Swiss inhabit which I won't name out of kindness to my father, who is the only one of us who ever goes there, taking with him a secretary and a thesis to write, and from which he comes down like Moses horned with good health and burdened with the Statistical Tables of the Economic Law to be a new covenant for the capitalists of the world, national and individual, in their devotion to the Golden Calf. He has long ceased, if he ever was, to be angry at the uses to which they put his pure reasoning, believing as I have heard him say at dinner that they would still be rogues without the knowledge he gives them but blundering, uninformed rogues who would cause panic and misery with their speculations and manipulations, where now they merely impede progress. It is, he often says, the difference between ducks and drakes and checkers. His own game is chess out of mathematics by ratiocination. My mother doesn't play games except liar dice. I wondered what games Ajax would play. I once had a six-week passion for mah-jongg: the complexity, the aesthetic pleasure of the pieces, the sensation of partaking of an ancient and refined evil akin to opium smoking, the legend that no Westerner should dare play it east of Suez. For those who don't know liar dice, I have of course maligned my mother by naming her favourite game; those who do will realize I mean it simply as a complimentary comment on her emotional subtlety.

It was still only just after dawn when we met at the airport. My father likes to make an early start. Given a choice between a comfortable hour and a Spartan one there is for him no choice. It's something to do with his Scandinavian Lutheranism combined with the long winter nights of his childhood. Grand'mère is the same. It requires great vigour of will to get up in the dark and go out into lamplit streets knowing that all the working day is ahead of you, that you must see the buildings washed with a chilling light and then blacken again before you can begin on your time. Each day becomes a Viking expedition into cold and dark. If you are to be strong, of the race of the berserkers, if you are to get up at all you get up quick and early; it is the first assault of the day. He is of course no longer a Lutheran, but the habits of thought are woven into him as the cadences of the English prayer book are into my disbelieving mother's speech. To lie abed is to tempt sin into the snuggled warmth of the blankets.

Through the glass door of the departure bay we could see the grey wastes of runway and field, the spent glow-worms of the runway lights pocking the edge of the carbon strip. Last night, I knew, they had glowed among all the other city lights that made a brilliant pectoral for a sleeping Titaness or a gemmed cloak for the Queen of the Night. A prone city on her back in flung disorder of blazing jewels is a most beautiful sight as you hover over her in your jet plane waiting to pitch down like Jove on Semele. But it was morning.

At that hour, behind that glass, people spoke quietly, almost reverentially whispered, as if in the presence of God as indeed they feared they might soon be. We are not yet used to the aeroplane, to wings. In spite of statistics we expect every time that our invention will fail us. We have an Icarus complex, as a species that is. We wish to fly to save time because our lives are so short that everything must be done as quickly as may be so that we can live as long as possible by density if not by extension. We wish to fly because we wish to be free of all the elements and we wish not to be bound by laborious space-time, the dragging of the worm's length across the surface of the soil, which was the nature of all travel until we were able to leap into the air and come down somewhere else. Yet we're afraid. It's unnatural. "If men had been intended to be birds God would have given them wings." We're afraid of our own pride, that GOD might choose this plane to smite us for our ingenuity and hubris since we have made him jealous in our own image and he hates anyone to try to reach him like the poor builders of the Tower of Babel, one of the nastier stories ever thought up for trying to keep us in our place and destroy our revolutionary and international aspirations. And now we have the rocket that may shoot us up from our earth womb free among the stars. Since we are Nature's, nothing we can conceive is unnatural. There is only Nobo Daddy to forbid us lest we should overreach him and grow up.

So we tremble in the departure bays of airports. The little man beside me with the thinning hair and the smart hide grip from which he would take documents to study in flight so that nemesis mightn't think he was enjoying it and punish him accordingly, rocked on his heels as I tried to count his eye-blink rate; the middle-aged wife with the jewelled Cleopatra eyeglasses clung to her husband's arm while he patted her hand absentmindedly. The door opened. The svelte hostess gave us our marching orders; there was no turning back now. The little man swallowed hard. I saw the bob of the Adam's apple. We moved forward in an orderly, silent file to dare fate.

"They are very beautiful," Ajax said.

"What?"

"Aeroplanes. The shape and the being made from metal make them beautiful. The rivets make them fragile and brave."

Was Ajax afraid? I looked for signs but I couldn't see any. I pictured my mother's lover,

"Hurld headlong flaming from th' Ethereal Skie,"

the yellow hair streaming back from the face as if in waves of poured bronze, Icarus-Phaeton-Lucifer, the rebel trinity of godsons, smiling as wings sprouted, great feathered vans that caught the tumbling figure and drifted it in cerulean reaches. I was a little surprised not to see them arcing above Ajax' head against the blue plastic cushion rest and wondered what the demure English hostess in her neat navy uniform would have said in place of: "Good morning ladies and gentlemen. On behalf of the captain and crew I should like to welcome you aboard. Would you please fasten your seat belts."

"Flying's still new enough to me for it to be exciting every time." Ajax clipped the two halves of the metal clasp together with an action as definite as buckling on a sword as portrayed in the late late cloak and dagger movies.

"I can't any longer remember my first flight," I said. "Why is it so exciting?"

"Sex and death I should think." My mother's lover had cleverly decided to treat me as an equal.

The jets sucked and spat us along the terrace. We rose until our gleaming cylinder shot off at the sky.

"Apotheosis," said Ajax. Looking out of the window I saw we were among clouds blushing and gilded with sun-rise and was unnerved to find them beautiful. I would be developing a taste for snowscapes next.

The plane put us down at Naples and we stepped into the hired car my father always had waiting at what-ever airport, the baggage was loaded, and we fled South through bougainvillaea, warm dust, and orange groves with "golden lamps in a green night" freed of their mat-ting blankets for the summer; then we were tunnelling through mountains or clinging to their sides with the coiled road, the land falling away in rocks and terraces and the sea sharp and far below almost inviting our plunge. My father drove precisely, magnificently, unruffled by the small-child tantrums of native drivers or the aggressive nervousness of tourists. Ajax sat beside him; my mother and I in back. Already my father had abandoned any at-tempt to flirt with or subjugate Ajax. Even the faint iras-cibility which I'd noticed in his voice on the occasion of Ajax' renaming had gone, replaced by the firm rationality he kept for his few equals. Sometimes I caught my mother's eyes watching them both in the stereo driving mirror.

Iticino, it is thought, was originally a Greek settlement, its name being ultimately derived from that nation's word for a fish, commuted by the Italians to a small fish, all the big ones having long since been speared, netted, lured with night lights to a surface doom and finally dynamited out of their waters so that all that remain are a few oversized and foolhardy squid drifted carelessly in from deeper seas and a multitude of bite-sized clams and prawns eked out by an occasional swarm of red mullet small enough for an ornamental pond or the celluloid playthings of a baby's bathtub. It was conquered successively by Saracens and Spanish, neither of whom could do anything with it, and last by certain tourists who were able to admire themselves as discriminating and susceptible to natural beauty in appreciating a spot too barren for any except the most pigheaded to think it worthwhile to hang on to. It has two rocky arms making a bay of sorts, a strip of beach where the boats are drawn up, the fishermen's wives' cottages (the men spending most of their time outdoors or in their own bar), and a shelving cliff clambered by Mediterranean foliage where the speculators have set the tourist villas. Halfway between the two worlds there is the piazza at which theoretically they might meet but of course never do, physical proximity being no guarantee of, in fact sometimes a discouragement to, even encounters let alone intimacy. Among themselves, the fishermen speak an unintelligible dialect which serves as a kind of thieves' cant while keeping one or two who are able to liaison for purposes of tapping off some of the visitors' molten stream in simple but pure Italian or even in an English backed by gestures learned from the movies as expected of them. There are two bars on opposite sides of the small piazza where each may observe and reflect on how the other half lives, its morals and mores, and come off with an equal measure of envy and self-righteousness. The colony fluctuates from summer to summer, the residents as far as one can judge stay the same but then Gennaro, old Arturo's son, may think the opposite from the lights of his bar as he peers across the dark cobbled square at the pale faces and hair above uniform T shirt and shorts of the men and women in the tourist stand and listens to their high-strung voices.

It would be foolish to imagine that the fishermen's way of life is any better than ours. It's time I said "ours" to make it quite clear where I stand or sit perhaps. It would be affected of me to try to pretend that I don't belong to my group as much as Gennaro to his. There is no such thing as the natural man except insofar as it is natural for man, of all the species, to be infinitely adaptable to his environment. The aborigine and the stockbroker are both natural men. I see no reason to envy Gennaro his so-called naturalness and in any case it has always seemed to me from observation that his group is as governed by cupidity (aptly derived from the Roman rather than the Greek god of love who at least gave us eroticism if nothing more) as my own. If I am terrified of us it is not because we are unnatural but because we are less defined. There is a hollow inside everyone but in most people it is cloaked and confined by their time and place; with us it seems to me that our thin coverings like the cotton shirts and shorts might too easily lift and blow away leaving nothing, while the fishermen sit on stolidly in their dark-blue sweaters and heavy trousers, their tanned ribbed feet anchored to the pavingstones, their hardwood hands clamped round thick tumblers. Maybe our lightness is a good thing. It could be that the fishermen are over-adapted, calcified but that we in our seeming evanescence are the next evolutionary mutation. Possibly it was the man less impeded by habit, time, and place who ran fast enough to escape the advancing ice age while the others nicknamed him Lightfoot, Will o' the Wisp, Young Shiftless. Now it is technology that advances gleaming and irresistible across the face of the earth, thrusting mankind out among the stars like an exploded peapod scattering seeds while we cling to our archaic social formulas hoping, cumbersome woolly-headed mammoths, to keep out relentless cold reason by growing thicker, cozier hides.

There is also a hotel del Golfo Azzurro which I'd forgotten because we have our own villa and so have never used it, but a room had been booked for Ajax there. My father hates hotels perhaps because he sees so many of them; that's why we have several residences. Our villa was built at the beginning of the boom and so is more solid than the later constructions of gravel blocks and cement washed in pastel shades like cubes of fudge set down behind the giant cacti. The windows are smaller; it is darker and cooler and more spacious with high ceilings and a loggia, and it is built of stone which gives an almost damp smell to the rooms, while the outside is crumbling in the heat so that to enter from the sunstricken landscape twitching and rustling with dry stalks and plastic leaves, chirr of cicadas and flicker of lizards, is to penetrate a moist twilit cave of silence, a labyrinth where you must feel your way or follow a thread of voice until your eyes and ears accustom themselves. But there isn't enough room for us all with Signora Gambardella and her daughter, who live there rent free in return for cooking and cleaning when we come to stay, not enough room for another one, and we have to have the Gambardellas because Fantah refuses to come to Iticino, saying that she feels like an outcast there. It's in vain that we explain that all Italians stare at everyone, ourselves included and that she is an exotic and an educational experience for them. Fantah has no proselytizing spirit.

My father drove first to the Albergo del Golfo and he and Ajax disappeared behind its inoffensive clean exterior, coffee fudge, while my mother and I sat on staring down at the view that gave the hotel its name until my father came out again and we began to drop down the hill.

"Not bad as these things go," he said. "Quite a good room with a balcony. I said to join us for dinner." My mother nodded. I pictured Ajax climbing up the hill at night and slapping down in the morning, feet smacking up little puffs of dust; lying in bed, staring at the ceiling and drawing on a cigarette. Did Ajax smoke? I couldn't remember. We drew up at our door. Signora Gambardella appeared miraculously, welcoming in the portal, herself a demand for painter and photographer who are unfortunately never around at annunciatory or apocalyptic moments.

"*Buon giorno, signori. Molto piacere.*" She stepped forward to help with the bags uneffusively but efficiently. We carried them into the villa where all was ready to greet us as my father remarked, bringing a deprecatory gesture from the signora with a little grimace. Out of the corner of my eye I saw a slim figure enter the salon.

"*Mia figlia!*" her mother indicated with obvious but controlled pride. I had known it must be but was still surprised. The stages in the development of the human tadpole may be plotted as accurately as those of any other animal and they occur at intervals of three years which may be called leap years, omitting the first baby year which is an extension of the wombtime. When we had last seen Renata she was a child of fifteen, now she was a woman of nearly seventeen.

Signora Gambardella was a foreigner from another province. Gambardella, if there ever had been one or if he had indeed sired Renata (there were so many possibilities), had long since disappeared and there was a marked and unusual reticence about "*mio marito.*" She was foreign to Iticino in every way. She spoke Italian, she wore light dresses in polished cotton or silk which didn't chime with her age or situation and she was educating her daughter, and her dowry, beyond the reach of the local sons. "*Parla inglese. Sarebbe utile per la pronuncia. È molto importante e difficile la pronuncia.*"

"How do you do?" said Renata calmly. She was very beautiful as young Italians are in their first, soon coarsened, bloom. She too, it seemed, had no intention of being trapped in Iticino. I wondered about the dowry and whether it would be enough to make a respectable catch on the open market. Her mother was the local witch or more precisely unofficial nurse and midwife. Whether she had any qualifications we never knew but her foreignness and seeming better education were enough. Many of the women preferred her for their own and their children's minor ailments and left gifts at the door, strangled chickens, eggs, fresh fish and fruit and propitiatory offerings. The doctor himself always asked for her assistance at confinements and was glad to be relieved of many small unremunerative demands on his aging skill and time. Maybe occasionally she even received money payments. Sometimes when we were staying there I would be wakened by a night summons under her window and in the morning there would be a slight bruising under her eyes and a little less youthfulness in her step but no complaint. My father had once made the mistake of suggesting she should go back to bed but this was countered with a "so sorry if he had been disturbed" that made him feel he had been prying.

Signora Gambardella was not a witch but she was unruffled in emergency and scrupulously clean. These two attributes not only made her powers of coping and healing seem miraculous, they endeared her to my father who liked his surroundings calm, ordered, and unsqualid although not positively antiseptic. I think my mother didn't notice as long as they were initially decorative and ugliness and dirt didn't become obtrusive enough to jut nastily into her dream world. Beautiful things attach themselves to her, group themselves around her as if consciously forming the background to a work of art and she is unaware, her face dreaming like Venus' lulled by the lute player whose notes fall unheeded as rain beyond the windows while away under the trees barely perceived figures leap and laugh in the gloom bagpiped to by a satyr. My mother is a work of art; every gesture, every inflection chosen long ago and refined by someone to whom Wilde's dictum of putting one's genius into life is a commonplace.

Dressed she is always *la grande dame*. When the bags had been stowed and we had exclaimed about the house and my father had noted that the chests of books and mechanical aids to composition had safely preceded us we had a light lunch washed down with the local white wine and slept while the heat poured into the ground like lava. Waking I went to the shuttered window, my bare feet happy to be cooled by the marbled floor, and looked down into the hot foliage of the garden that had withstood another afternoon and would soon sink gratefully into a dark as deep as that of a photographer's black hood. The husband of one of the signora's most regular customers tended it for her, giving her all its fruits in season: figs, peaches, grapes, *fichi d'India*, tomatoes, squashes, melons. I turned away and began to shower and dress. I wanted to be down first and standing at the foot of the stairs for her descent.

It was Odette (or should I say Madame Swann? Perhaps both, the total experience being incomplete without either part) walking in the Bois though attended only by my father two stairs behind. The air within the long oblong frame of the stair well seemed full of small invisible wings. Yet this is sleight of hand, the barge she sat in. I should re-create her for you at that moment but I can't perhaps because almost at once I was aware that someone stood behind me at my shoulder and turned and saw that Ajax had come in through the open front door and was gazing up too. My mother is of course infinitely more intelligent than Madame Swann; I make the comparison only to give some impression of the size of the occasion. It might perhaps be thought wrong to liken one's mother to a courtesan who had but recently gained respectability by marrying her lover but you should know enough of me by now to realize that it is one of my brilliant two-edged compliments. Indeed it was her long apprenticeship that made Odette worth anything. Had she been born and early married into status she would have been nothing. Her striving was an act of the imagination. And there is the difference. My mother's whole being is an act of the imagination. She doesn't even draw breath spontaneously as other people do but as a willed art as one might play an oboe. Her dress was some kind of gauze in art nouveau blue and green, dark and lustrous like old brooches made from butterfly wings or paua shell, delphinium mother of pearl. Was that the moment when Ajax fell in love?

At dinner we were waited on by Renata and her mother. I saw my father growing restive. It had been one thing to be served by the signora who had let it be known that any other arrangement would be a deep affront and by the child Renata, to whom he could give pocket money in recompense, but the cool young woman roused the egalitarian in him and he was unable to adjust his attitudes quickly enough. Instead of the smile that used to let charm fall on the child's head like a blessing he scowled and muttered a *grazie* totally without grace to the proffered dish of green beans. Maybe Renata had noticed his gruffness or maybe she had decided she was an egalitarian too for she didn't reappear with the dessert and as the wine went round the table my father began to relax and become the benevolent magnetic public presence we were all used to.

They all drank a great deal. My father's puritanism does not extend to drink. He retains his Old World need for alcohol with meals which indeed the New World might have had if the first discoverers had been settlers too. Not for nothing did they call it Vinland. A land flowing with milk and honey is all very well as long as you know how to ferment them both, but wild grapes are better. The primordial kick like a mule must have been from mare's milk no doubt drunk by my father's ancestors. On reflection I suppose they must be mine too. It's strange how undescended I feel in relation to both my parents; more like a changeling as though I had simply chosen the two most interesting people in the world to come and stay with. I have none of the sticky feeling of the same blood flowing in our veins. Then again I find it very difficult to think of Grand'-mère as my father's mother probably because she has never insisted on such a chain of begetting. When she was young she knew the aging Ibsen and may have learnt from him about visiting the sins and the virtues of the fathers upon the children. The stories Grand'-mère told me when I was small were all the entirely suitable Teutonic and Scandinavian folk and fairy tales of death and passion that feed a child's imagination without burdening it as family history may. With my parents she is polite and dignified. All this is to explain that I don't feel my father's ancestors to be mine though curiously I do feel they are his. There are some people who carry about with them the aura of another period almost as if they had leapt a time span and landed in our century. You will see from this that I also don't think there is any other era that would have accommodated me. My mother might be late Roman—that flowering of consciousness historians label decadence. She has an excellent late Roman head too—for drink. My father is a sea wolf.

We began frozenly enough even without the difficulty with Renata and my father's principles. On such occasions of social strain my mother ducks her beautiful head down to her plate and prays that the cup may pass from her. I wondered how Ajax would cope and began on my antipasto with a concealed delight that had nothing to do with the signora's arrangement of tasty and colourful mouthfuls. "You chatter like the Bandar-Log," Baloo says to little frog Mowgli, who is being trained by that grizzled Arnold of Rugby (with the aid of General Bagheera and financier Kaa) in the public school Jungle to be a leader of men and must on no account be sullied by contact with the feckless, dirty, garrulous, undeserving underapes. In common with our monkey cousins we have inherited a social pattern in which the weaker propitiate the stronger with soothing noises and offers of services. In our species money takes the place of physical strength. Underdogs chatter; not only individuals but whole groups; Jews carrying the ghetto loquacity up into the Manhattan power seats; women; the industrial proletariat, but not the rural peasantry, who aren't in direct confrontation with the aggressor often enough, and professional jesters of all kinds. Between ape and angel is Homo vulgaris, the clown, a word that's always had two meanings. Ajax chattered and gradually I was aware that my mother was no longer just

sheltering behind the flow; she was listening, for her silence isn't arrogance as such usually are but a breakdown
in the necessary confidence that what we have to say is
worth attention. Ajax spieled, pattered, manipulated unseen puppets, drew scenes and characters with a charla-
tan's fluency. Then my mother's lover began to question
deftly, provoking answers from them both. My mother sat
up, my father laughed and passed the carafe. It was a good
performance; I nearly applauded. I wondered if Ajax was
sweating with fear and exertion. I could see the thin shirt
clinging to the untanned flesh. Perhaps it was just the heat
of the wine.

"This time," said my father, "I'm going to try something new and I want you all to help me. I wish to make a
book of ideas."

"Is that new?" I said taking a breadstick and snapping
it into three lengths to make the letter K.

"Yes and no." He is always unruffled by my cheek.
"This will be a Socratic dialogue."

"No figures?" I rearranged the breadstick into a squat
A.

"Very few. It will be a symposium."

"With wine?" I looked up to see whether Ajax had
taken my mother's point but was unable to judge from the
smiling attentiveness. It was as though having at last got
the actors to move Ajax held them to their parts by a supreme concentration of the will.

"If we need it. I am bored with figures. They only tell
people what they want to know or rather they take the
figures and shrink them to their little purposes. Like
Malthus. If I tell them their population will be doubled

by the end of the century they wonder where they can buy more food not how they can stop it doubling. It is perhaps time to state a few things in obvious terms."

"Why do you need us?"

"Perhaps to sharpen my own ideas, perhaps because it will be more interesting if it is a discussion. In one of those cases which came before us is a tape recorder."

"We shall need the wine then."

"You find them inhibiting?" Ajax leaned forward to offer her a light from the ritual candle the signora always placed on the altar table.

"Very." She drew in deeply and they looked at each other through the flame.

"So shall I. I shall have to type from one."

"Is it to be verbatim," my mother asked, "with the pauses and incoherencies?"

"No. Ajax and I will edit and select. It will be as smooth as Plato."

"And as rational?"

He moved his shoulders in the international gesture of who knows. "Maybe. We must try. We will have either false names or just initials. Character is not necessary only to differentiate the distinct points of view."

"So it doesn't matter," said Ajax, "whether we believe what we say or not? It's possible to play devil's advocate for the sake of advancing the argument?"

"Yes, that would be so."

"But don't we think as we do because of what we are?" my mother asked her lover across the Hellespont of the table.

"Shush," said my father. "We are beginning already

you see and the tape recorder isn't working. Besides we are all too tired. Tomorrow we will start."

"Wilde did it once or twice didn't he?" asked Ajax.

"*The Critic As Artist* you mean? Yes, that's a Socratic dialogue. If our arguments could be as cogent and as beautiful as that the result would be a work of art." My mother flicked her head so that the long hair flowed back from her face and I heard an inaudible snort of self-derision.

"We might invite Renata to join us sometimes. It would be good for her English." My father pushed back his chair. "Shall we walk down to the piazza? It should be cooler there. I will tell the signora not to bother with coffee."

My mother put on a light coat and we went down the cobbled lane through the rich dark. The piazza was puddled on two sides with light from the opposing bars like the moonlit mudbanks between the black river whose waves were the unending procession of linked bodies, the young men and girls as fanatically separated as in an old-style New England Sunday school yet so aware of each other that the spaces between the chained crests were thick with the ripples of consciousness. We took our place in the half empty bar; it was too early in the season yet for the full tourist flood.

"You must try the local firewater, *anice*, a sort of crude pernod. The fishermen drink it neat with hot coffee on cold mornings if you can imagine there ever being such a thing on a night like this. I can't tempt you, darling, can I?"

My mother shook her head. "What about Kit?"

"Yes, I'd like one." I wanted to add the water and have the illusion of drinking absinthe, green milk of sin drawn from the devil's dam, Hecate of the wry tits. Gennaro would be drinking a milksop cappuccino in the belief that anything stronger would harm his nerves or stomach. I strained my eyes across the river to pick him out but he wasn't there. At least it seemed to me that the boy sitting with the fishermen was quite different from the one I'd known before. I peered into the ceaseless ebb and flow of bodies, thinning now of girls so that only the *giovanotti* were left.

"*Hue Gennar'. Du sta la vedova staser'?*" One of the men called from the table. A slim boy on the end of a line of three turned and grinned.

"*Lan goppa la, a letto,*" he called back.

"*Va su, va su!*" The men broke into theatrical laughter. Gennaro had crossed the line like Renata. Suddenly there was silence. Two figures of women had come into the square arm in arm, stepping in time, heads held up but not aggressively high. My father stood up and bowed. "*Prego signora, s'accomodi. Qualche piccola cosa a bere?* What would you like, Renata?" He waved them to our table. The signora bowed back in gracious acceptance.

"My mother would like a white cinzano and I a Scotch on the rocks with some soda, please. Thank you. It is most kind."

I was aware of a guitar twanging into the silence and American voices. A group had seated themselves at one of the tables taking the limelight from us for a moment. The signora pursed her mouth.

"Who are they?"

"They are people of nothing. They don't work. They are, *come si dice*—boums?"

"Bums," I said with great pleasure.

"*Robaccia!*" said the signora who always understood more than one expected.

"They sleep on the beach," said Renata. "They make fires."

"Students," I said. Renata and her mother looked sceptical. "Or hippies," I added.

"Ah!" They had read about them in the papers. "What means 'hippy'?" Renata asked.

"To be hip," Ajax offered, "is to be not concerned with society and its conventions."

Renata translated for her mother who pursed her lips even more. The guitarist began to sing again.

> "Come all you fair and tender ladies,
> Be careful how you court young men.
> They're like a star of a summer morning;
> They'll first appear and then they're gone."

Ajax looked at my mother. "It's interesting how the conventions shift sex from one age to another."

"How do you mean?"

"Perhaps I mean concepts rather than conventions. The Elizabethans thought women the fickle sex.

> "Just such disparity
> As is twixt Air and Angels' purity
> Twixt women's love, and men's will ever be."

"Is that true? 'Men were deceivers ever'?"

"On balance I think it's probably true and the last time it was; a combination of the cult of a virgin queen and the remnants of courtly love."

"And since then?" I swirled my cloudy glass.

"I would have thought the seventeenth and eighteenth centuries kept them pretty much equal. What do you think, Renata?"

"Oh, men are always . . . how do you say?"

"Fickle?"

"Yes. Fickle."

"*Cosa?*" the signora asked rather sharply. Renata seemed to have some difficulty in explaining.

"Doesn't your mother agree?" my father asked.

"She thought I say something different—a bad word."

"Are there any bad words?" my mother asked of no one in particular.

The signora and Renata rose to go. Stiff-backed, unseeing, they stalked through the promenaders while the voices murmured about them and the guitar put in a ground swell.

I was up early next morning but my father was there before me unpacking the cases. In Iticino we breakfast separately since there are no morning papers to bind us together. My mother sleeps later. I ate a roll and butter washed down with milky coffee and then went out into a street already warm and slightly hazy with sucked up dew. My first expedition in Iticino was always to buy *zoccoli*, the wooden soles with a leather thong that everyone wore to clatter over the beach and down the hard streets. At first the tender feet blister in protest but gradually they become calloused with salt and sun and unflinching wear. It's the nearest I've found to an Indian initiation rite or those endurance feats the young Felix Krull engaged in. I know it's childish but the pain gives me pleasure.

The small market in the piazza was already in chattering swing. My feet had grown two sizes since last year and I bought two pairs, one of wood and one of rubber for when my flesh began to bleed. Swinging the rubber ones I went on down between the fishermen's cottages towards the beach where the boats were already drawn up drying and one or two fishermen lounged, the older ones mending torn netting, holding the mesh taut between bare toes and knotting and looping the coral thread from the wooden shuttle with the unconscious deftness of Belgian women at their lace pillows while they dribbled the unintelligible syllables out of salt-swollen lips. As I left the group behind I felt the syllables and the sunken discoloured whites of their eyes slide over me as if I were drowned deep and they an animated and devouring slime on my flesh. I almost shivered in the heat. If they could have done without them they would have wrapped the tourists in their nets and sunk them out beyond the harbour but they had grown used to the additional comforts the tourists brought and they could no longer live at the simple level of their fathers. In the state of dazed semi-consciousness that attends being alone and stared at by a hostile group I walked on along the beach.

Two arms enclose the tiny harbour which is no more than a strip of beach; one arm is manmade—a concrete mole with a miniature lighthouse, the other is natural rock, on one side lapped by the sea at its base, on the other with caves and patches of sand as if a child had made a dwarf parody of the real coast. The two pairs of sandals and most of my clothes I left behind a rock on a doll-size Palm Beach and stepped into the caress of the water. It was always delicious this first encounter. Maybe that was how sex would be, might be, I amended to myself. With Jude it had been cold, almost disembodied. The mind had watched the body writhe. There was more involvement in making love to oneself, for one was both singer and song. I pushed through the shallows and off free into the clear still water as though into a lachrymatory filled with warm brine of a beautiful mistress' tears. Hair of weed caught at me and flowed enticingly away from the thrust of my legs. Steadily I worked my way along the spur. At the tip there would be strong currents before I turned into the next bay. The slight but real element of danger pleased me; I like to frighten myself a little. Already I could feel the pull of them as they tried to keep me from rounding the point and swing me out to sea. Aware that I was still soft I fought them back with arms and legs, resisting the desire to stroke faster which would only mean weaker and involve a quicker loss of strength. Deliberately I kept my rhythm. This too was always, like the sensation of entering the water, something I looked forward to in the first bathe on each of our repeated visits to Iticino: the fear, the struggle, the mastering of one's own mind and body and the moment of panic, the whiff of death in the nostrils like the tangy suspicion of a fall bonfire far away, scented but not seen. I rounded my own particular Horn and felt the waters begin to pull with me towards the shore.

Some way out still I paused and rolled onto my back to rest and survey the shore. I had known this was where they must be, and sure enough there were the anonymous bundles lying like logs or pigs of lead, sometimes singly, sometimes bulkily signifying a couple. At one end of the beach was a tent. Only one person seemed to be up, moving slowly along in search of driftwood which he presently brought back to the blackened site of last night's fire. By the time I had turned over and slowly made my way through the shallows til my legs grounded and I could rear up out of the sea like Father Tiber from his riverbed instead of wallowing ignominiously landwards with soles wincing at every pebble and shell, he had got the fire blazing as merrily as a boy scout. Fingering the salt drops out of my eyes I walked towards him. It was St. Gelbert's all over again. I wondered how long before he would either offer me a smoke or ask if I had any.

The squatting figure looked up: "You're blocking out my sunlight." It was the guitarist.

"I thought the great thing about it was that it was free."

"So take a piece somewheres else."

"You play a cool guitar." I looked away from him and out towards the sea. Coffee began to bubble succulently in an aluminium can.

He grunted and poked at the fire. "Ain't you afraid to be up so early?"

"I always get up early here. Maybe it's the heat." I waited for the next thrust.

"Come here often as the brothel keeper said to the bishop?"

I crouched down on the sand at the other side of the fire. "Every year."

"You from the States?"

"I'm from nowhere," I said.

"That's right: that's how it ought to be. You want some coffee?" He held out a paper cup.

"Thanks."

"Sugar's in that packet. Watch out for the ants. They get into everything worse than termites."

I picked an uncaught twig from the edge of the smouldering heap, bleached and scoured like a rabbit's bone found in the woods, and stired the hot black liquid. An ant scrambled up a snowslope and was tumbled back and buried under a sudden sweet avalanche. I dug it out with the dry end of stick and put it to safety on the sahara of the beach.

"Makes you feel like God and if you spat you could drown it." He gobbed impressively at the sea. "How'd you get here?"

"Swam round the point. Always do first morning we're here to see if I still can."

"You stay in a hotel or one of them crummy villas?"

"The crummiest; the oldest. My old man can't stand hotels."

"Wise guy." For a moment we sat and mouthed the coffee in what is called companionable silence but is really a test of nerve where it isn't indifference.

"They ever get up?" I jerked my head at the stranded whales.

"When I kick them."

"And that?" I nodded at the ramshackle teepee.

"Oh, we call that Honeymoon Hotel, for them that want to take their clothes off for each other. The natives round here ain't very sophisticated."

I laughed and stood the cup deliberately in the hot embers so that the heat reached up for my hand and the waxed paper wept and charred, popped into flame and was left in charcoal skeleton. Then I got up. "I have to go. Thanks for the coffee."

He put up a hand. "Leo," he said.

"Kit."

"See you."

"See you." I walked back into the sea, knowing he was watching my arse, and struck off as soon as I could. There was no depth for a running dive and anyway I might have belly-flopped. Calculated strokes drove me at the point; I let the current take me out a little and round, more sure of myself now. Half a dozen strong thrusts dragged me out of its grave pull. I swam slowly back to my clothes and stretched out on the rock to dry, falling briefly but deeply asleep in the hot shade of the overhang.

"Where have you been?" asked my father without urgency but as a greeting as I'd hoped he would.

"Interviewing Diogenes," I said and went on up to shower.

"Let us first pour a libation to the dead," said my father filling our post-lunch glasses while the twin wheels of the tape recorder whispered to each other in the corner and the green Polyphemus eye winked at his words.

"Which of the dead are we honouring?" asked my mother.

"Philosophy, that ancient Sibyl with her shameful rags gathered about her."

"I've always imagined her like Michelangelo's Sistine Sibyl: a great coarse body containing the worst elements of both sexes," Ajax said, watching the winking light for volume.

"That's it exactly. She was a hybrid, put together of many things." Sometimes my father's English is a little strange.

"And her death is a matter of falling apart into the constituent elements each one of which becomes a science, a study in itself."

"Exactly so. Cosmology, psychology, economics, sociology, biology, physics are all the offspring of her dissolution."

"She was a Titaness in fact," Ajax offered, "and from her blood new monsters spring up."

"They may be very beautiful," I put in. "Aphrodite was born in much the same way."

"Which one would you equate with Aphrodite?" my mother asked.

"Cosmology is very beautiful but in too distant a way, much like the music of the spheres."

"The modern picture we have of the universe is in fact as magnificent as its pre-scientific counterpart, if anything more so, which is unusual. The increase of knowledge tends to lessen our sense of grandeur as a rule. Mystery is an essential to worship."

"Is it because our knowledge is in that partial state,

the crusaders' first view of Jerusalem? Perhaps as we know more it'll become as commonplace to us as the moon's rock."

"Perhaps the only ultimate mystery and therefore fit subject of worship is another person because it's the one thing we can never completely know, never completely assimilate," said Ajax.

"But is the person worth knowing?" My mother sipped at the unpoured libation without looking up. "Is there anything either mysterious or beautiful in another human being? Most people are as seizable as objects."

"A person may be like a work of art which even if you hang on your wall you don't possess."

"That would be a very rare person."

"Yes, most rare."

"So," said my father, "the mystery of the sciences is only beautiful as long as our knowledge is partial. The moon once landed upon becomes a chunk of rock and we must go on to Venus which in its turn we shall suck dry of its secrets, digest and discard. Is it then worthwhile to go on since knowledge leads inevitably to disenchantment?"

"It's an academic question. We have no choice. Short of blowing up the world we can't stop."

"You mean each step is inherent in the one before?" my mother asked.

"Yes, even if I refuse to go on with my piece of research someone, somewhere will go on with it."

"Civilisation has failed before."

"But even then not completely, if you mean the Dark Ages," I objected.

"It may have been a necessary period of cross-pollination," said Ajax.

My mother frowned. She is, as I've said, late Roman and the first millennium A.D., a long winter of her discontent given over to superstition and violence.

"Certainly the contraction of the world by technology makes it, as Kit says, virtually impossible to stop our advance without the destruction of the world. If Europe, Russia, and America were destroyed Africa and Asia would carry on the progress with only the briefest of hiccups. Therefore," said my father, "we have to accept the gradual discovery and assimilation of all fact: an evolution as inevitable as the biological predecessor of which indeed it is only the extension. And yesterday's discovery is tomorrow's commonplace." He was in full flight, but at this moment the tape recorder screamed an irresistible protest. Ajax fell upon it and silenced its complaint. "Is there any limit to what we can know?" my father began again.

"I can't see any," Ajax looked up from the censorious robot. "Not to what we can know."

"Then to our eventual satiation and boredom?"

"The human quest for knowledge is a form of addiction," said my mother, "insatiable and yet satiating. Unless fresh things are being created for us to discover there must, however distant, be a conceivable end, and because conceivable, real, now."

"Science then can't be an end in itself since it's got an end even though from our partial standpoint it's hard to see. And the same with its applications: the conquest of all the world's material ills can be foreseen so though they're a necessary means they can't be an end."

"An end can only be something without an end, something inexhaustible then," I said.

"We have arrived at a paradox."

"Surely that's just playing with words," my mother objected. "Insofar as science is simply discovery it isn't illimitable, that's all we're saying."

"Then what is?" my father sounded a little piqued.

"Creation."

"Any animal can create," I said.

"No; it can reproduce."

"If you leave out God," said Ajax, "which I take it we all do, then creation is man's prerogative."

"What about creation in the universe?" my mother asked.

"As far as we know it's mechanical and inevitable. Put two atoms of hydrogen and one of oxygen together and bang: it's water. We shall probably find the same is true of the origin of life. In time we'll be able to create new human beings just as Shaw and the science fiction writers have forecast for fifty years. What is strange is that our perception of the shape of the future is so much in advance of our emotional ability to cope with it." My father drew deeply on his glass as if it might give some answer.

"You mean," said Ajax, "that certain talented and intelligent people tell us what will happen and like Cassandra aren't believed as we continue as if we were living in the Middle Ages. The depression between the wars like some medieval famine . . ."

"The paranoia of Hitler's Jew-hunting," said my father, "like the madness of witch-hunting."

"Half a century of disease, hunger, violence . . ." My mother took up the litany, "and now at last when we begin to make technological progress it seems as if we're emotionally exhausted by a series of deathly orgasms and want only comfort."

"Maybe we just moved from childhood to old age without any prime," I said.

There was a thick silence in the room while outside the dry heat crackled and the insects made mindless noise.

You will be wondering, putative reader, why I have reported all this. The answer is quite simple: it interests me and you, forgive me, don't. I am not trying to tell you anything; I am at my childlike, priestlike task of creation. I am building sand castles for the tide to wash away or making mudpies that will never be eaten. You are privileged, if you ever exist, to look over my shoulder and study my re-creation but you mustn't interfere with your chatter about what you like. I warned you that I have the privileges of a child still and you can't rule my games, for to tell you the truth you adults disgust and bore me and perhaps frighten me too with your terrible unreflecting power. You want nothing but the story and then you complain because people like me prefer nonfiction: tracts, flower poems, plainchant, as if epic, romance, saga, novel hadn't always been the fit place for all these things. But I have my models, Felix and Marcel, my gemini saints. It is the geometry against which the man in the background is taking off his shirt that I have given you, and it establishes the perspective of that man and the protagonists busy with their initiation rite in the foreground. I shall do it again, I warn you, because it excites and interests me and because even by your own uncurious, unwarped standards of unimagination it is true. You want only the man taking off his shirt, naked humanity you would call it and the common touch, but I shall report the gossip of angels, the symbolic actions of mythical figures, the tree that is more than natural, that is a columnal àrch: a piece of architecture because without them the naked man might as well have kept his shirt on, without them he is simply inviting a commonplace cold. On the very simplest level you would ask me to pretend that people don't think and talk except in the monosyllables of cliché. You say that when I am older I shall forget all this speculation and settle down to the important practical concerns of life; perhaps that's why among adults I find my parents the most interesting people in the world. They have their faults: my father, for example, as you will have noticed, is inclined to be ponderous and lecture to an audience of one, but they don't bore me with materialism. You will say too that if they were poor and untalented it would be a different story: that is to say that if the combustion engine hadn't been invented we should have still been travelling muleback and that it would somehow be virtuous in us to do so now. I reject all this in my rejection of your desire that I should feed you with a rapid fire of dramatic and pungent moments to give you the illusion of action. It is inartistic; it's untrue and it bores me. Enough.

"I refuse to be old before my time," said my mother's lover. "There must be another answer." The tape recorder clattered an empty spool in agreement and Ajax switched it off. My mother looked up curiously at this display of vehemence. Ajax stood very taut as if for running and it was then I think that the difference between my mother's lover and the rest of us struck me and perhaps her. We are not at home in our bodies or at least my father and I aren't. We shuffle them on in the morning with our clothes. My mother has taken hers and moulded it felinely to her. Ajax was that body; informed it without any suggestion of ghost in the machine.

"Well," said my father, "we have made a beginning, a very interesting one. Let us pause there as the mechanism suggests."

I went through into the kitchen to fetch a drink of water. As I opened the door or rather gave it a preliminary rattle of the handle I heard a voice say, *"Scostumad', vatene!"* but when I got inside there was only Renata sitting at the formica covered table in front of the window an open book in front of her. She seemed to look up. I smiled.

"Ho sete." I explained. *"Dov'è la signora?"*

"My mother is out," she answered, determined to practise.

"Oh. What's the book?"

"It is for the Cambridge Proficiency Exam. It's called *Tom Sawyer*. It's about a boy Tom and his friend Uck. You know it?"

"Oh yes I know it."

"Are all American boys like this?"

"Like what?"

"So young, so naughty?"

"It's a bit old-fashioned."

"How?"

"All'antica. Di cento anni fa."

"It is not like the films."

"No," I drew my glass of water from the sink beside the window, glancing quickly out as I did so. Was it imagination or did the big tree conceal a serpent in the signora's garden? "Good luck," I said lifting the glass.

"*Come?*"

"With the book."

"Oh yes, thank you."

I went back into the salon in time to hear my father saying: "If you'd like to take the car . . ."

"Won't you come too?"

"No. I would like some tea and some rest. I'm not yet acclimatized to the heat I think. Signora Gambardella can make me some tea."

"She's out. Renata's in the kitchen."

"Then I shall teach her how to make tea." My father, as they say, brightened visibly and contrived to at once look younger than his age. I tossed up which would be the more sport: to stay at home and listen or to go abroad and watch. With me out of the way my father would have every chance to bring his aspirations to a more interesting point and I was anxious to observe Ajax driving. There are so few activities left to us in which we can express ourselves or give ourselves away. Driving, the most common, is also, fortunately, most revealing. And I wanted Ajax to notice me.

"Kit?" my mother queried.

"I'll come with you if I may?"

"Of course, darling."

"I'll just go and change and then I'll come and collect you," Ajax said taking the keys from my father's outstretched hand. My mother nodded and went upstairs.

Then I heard my father go through into the kitchen feigning surprise, the slam of the car door and the engine firing and drawing away. I wondered if the fig tree was barren of its strange fruit by now.

My mother's lover came back with the effulgence of one newly bathed and deodorized. The car when we got into it had that faint cosmetic fragrance of cleanliness. Ajax was wearing white reefer trousers like an enlisted sailor and a purple T shirt that showed up the muscled arms with their "broth of goldfish blue breathed round." My mother (have I told you? I forget, anyhow it's so unusual that an offspring should think so that it's worth repeating) is very beautiful (but then beauty is in the eye of the beholder; most children are in competition with their parents and so can't find them beautiful or feel themselves derived and therefore need to be able to lay the charge of their own ugliness, for we're most of us ugly to ourselves, firmly on the genes). With neither of these disabilities I'm able to see my parents, my father's rather heavy handsomeness and my mother's grace, without prejudice. On this day she was wearing one of her many shades of blue shot with purple or green in a clinging artificial silk, since she won't wear real silk, fur or leather. I remember a fraught Christmas when Grand'mère sent us all reindeer skin slippers because she'd read that New York was in the grip of a blizzard and was sure that only the natural product would be good enough to keep the cold away, and even my mother's built-in good manners had been unable to overcome her repugnance as she lifted them firmly from their wrapping. They were never worn. On her the false looked real. Her clothes, bought all over the world wherever something caught her eye, were always cheap yet appeared affluent with that right simplicity that is traditionally supposed to cost a fortune. She has gone to a diplomatic dinner party in Singapore in a housecoat bought in a London chainstore and outshone them all without even a piece of jewellery to distract from it or tart it up in any way. It was as if the ersatz took a certain truth from her and became echt. Every day as a simple miracle one could say she made water into wine.

We got into the car, Ajax and my mother in front, me behind, and climbed the steep road out of town—Ajax taking it firmly but steadily. The run up and down to change had also brought a little unspied-on experience with a strange machine.

"If you note a tendency in me to drive on the wrong side of the road remind me," Ajax said. My father finds England the wrong side since Sweden went Right. It set Ajax apart as a more located person. We took the opposite direction from the one we had come to Iticino from, along the coast southward. "What happens along here?"

"A few wartime battlefields farther on," my mother offered, "if they interest you."

Ajax gave a mock shudder. "In any case I should think they're all overgrown by now. You could work out how the battle was fought I suppose if you stood on a hill; a bit like a general planning strategy."

"Is war never for you?"

"I acknowledge the attractions but they have to be resisted."

"Anyway you don't come to battlefields yet," I put in. "There's quite a bit of winding coast first."

So we wound a white road between blue sea and sky indistinguishable from each other against a rocky cliff, sentineled by huge cacti.

"We could stop for a bit if you'd like," said my mother. Sometimes there was a kind of natural observation platform jutting over the sea above a tiny village less than Iticino that somehow netted a living from a fissure in the rocks and a scattering of volcanic soil shepherded into minute terraces. "What about here?"

Ajax swung the car sharply off the road so that it stood as if on a broad plinth facing out to sea and switched off the engine. Nobody spoke. After the vibration of our passage it seemed almost as if we were holding our breath and then the chirrup of cicada and the heat began to seep through the open windows.

"There might be more air outside," said Ajax. My mother fumbled with the door but got the window winder by mistake. While I watched her not quite realizing her confusion, Ajax opened the driver's door, got out, and came round the front of the Fiat. As my mother's lover levered the handle my mother looked up. There wasn't even the decency of glass between their eyes. She got out.

It isn't often that one is privileged to observe this moment so that afterwards one can pinpoint it exactly and say, "Yes, that was it." My mother walked, rather shakily I suspect, towards the edge of the platform, Ajax following.

When we are living on the farm in Massachusetts and I tire of fishing I take a quick plane to New York to inhale the city. I wander it from end to end anonymous as any other child, sometimes stopping to watch games of baseball behind a wire mesh, curious though unenvious of

other children absorbed together, but most often tracking
the vast grey halls of the Metropolitan Museum, joining
the file with my lunch tray and sitting down beside the
fountain, with its monstrous Etruscanesque ironware figures rushing gaily to nowhere, and waiting to see what delight of chance and dotty companionship will veer towards
my table. In one of the rooms hangs a splendid Veronese,
Cupid binding the legs of Venus and Mars in a lover's
knot. I have known what it is to play that Cupid, to give a
blessing to my mother and her lover at their onset of
union. They are figures of great richness and stature, dam-
asked, armoured though she has cast hers, the Don and
Donna of some High Renaissance *favola* that Shakespeare
didn't have time to use. It didn't matter that Ajax'
clothes clung with sweat, moulding buttocks and thighs
like a second skin. Venus' forehead, could we feel it, is
probably damp too, the hair certainly a little distrait. It
seems as if she blushes and modestly lowers her gaze, os-
tensibly to the officious boy while squeezing a milky and
compensatory pearl from her breast. Mars too looks round
startled and perhaps a little frightened, who never feared
before; at the slender yet steely pink ribbon that binds him,
precursor of that invisible net in which he will be en-
snared. My mother and Ajax stood looking down at tumbling hillside, sea, and rocks. As I walked towards them the
magnetic field of their lust was so strong it seemed almost
a visible cloud that might rise with them and bear them
out to sea.

Briefly I wondered how my father was doing. However I had no regrets. This was a bonus I hadn't expected.
I could soon catch up on the home news: Jupiter and An-

tiope. Ajax was saying something about the view. My mother nodded and asked if Ajax had been this far south before. "At Rome modern times begin. Below is somehow still classical. Nothing that has happened since has really impinged on the landscape. It's not an original thought any more than the suggestion that Stonehenge in England is terrifying; it just seems to me true."

"The country of myth," I said coming up behind them. And now the Fiat had become Venus' triumphal car, the wheels sprouted feathers of white dust along the road and the charioteer spun a gold circle like a sun disc. If I don't feel myself greatly my parents' child I do, maybe more so because of that, feel myself the inheritor of civilisation. My imagination is stuffed with the legends of the world, mainly the Western world of course though the East has given its share too in Babylon and China and, by extension, Mohawk and Apache and Christian myth, like a pirates' hoard or Arabian nights' treasure. At any moment I can open my store and gloat in secret over its jewels and time-untarnished finery. I find them more evocative than the synthetic *diamanté* of our own time: war heroes and movie stars acting out the same legends I have observed on some great canvas in the Prado or heard at La Scala. Perhaps I have something of my father's sense of time, combined with my mother's sense of immediacy so that all I've seen and read as we've gone about the world has become the furniture of my mind as usual to me as chairs and neighbours are to other children. I wouldn't have put it so at St. Gelbert's any more than Jude revealed her music but I suspected that every child there harboured a private mythology in its own head that it would later become ashamed of. My parents I know have theirs and aren't ashamed but most adults are conditioned out of fancy into the practical, into numbed lives. So it was natural to me to have seen that triumphal car and its occupants in those terms, to give them the dignity of art, as Homer did small-town Helen, who ran off with a visitor (hired hand, commercial traveller?) and was chased by an irate husband at the head of a posse of kinfolk and neighbours, though it was only in my own head that the picture might be hung or the words imprinted.

The house when we reached it was very quiet and no one appeared in answer to the sound of the car drawing up or the closing of the front door and our voices. There was still some time before dinner. Surprisingly the drive had been relatively short, though I felt as exhausted as if we'd been out all day. For a moment my mother stood hesitating in the hall. "Would you like a drink? What are you going to do, darling?"

"I swam a long way this morning; I'm rather tired. I think I'll take a sleep."

She turned to Ajax again and looked her question.

"I ought to shower and change. Driving in this heat soaks me through I'm afraid."

"I haven't seen your room. Is it nice?"

"I could give you a drink there if you didn't mind amusing yourself while I get ready."

"That would be nice. I feel a little guilty about your being in a hotel. I'd like to reassure myself that it isn't too squalid."

I smiled inwardly at their attempts to deceive themselves, each other and me, waved a weary but cheerful goodbye and watched from an upstairs window while they went out and got into the car without touching or speaking. The car roared away up the hill. I went into my own room, tore off my also damp clothes and lay down on the cool sheet that was almost instantly fever moist and hot from my body; I rolled onto another patch to repeat the cooling. What were they doing now? They had escaped me and always would unless I could find a way to see without being seen. I slid a hand over the wet curls of my crotch and began to caress myself slowly. The room was like the exotic tropical hothouse of a botanical gardens, dim and steamy, and myself a fleshy orchid, parasite on others' emotions; or a venus fly trap I thought and laughed and squirmed with simultaneous pleasures. It is hard to be young: our imaginations are as hot as eunuchs' and our opportunities for satisfying them almost as rare as theirs. Sometimes I have to bolt myself in my room or the john and toss off four or five times a day. As I fell asleep I wondered where my father and Renata were but I was too tired to do anything about that now. Later dimly I thought I heard the car come back. I must find some way but warmth and delicious weariness flowed over me again blotting out the impulse to go to the head of the stairs and watch their entrance.

Renata didn't appear at dinner. My father said that Ellie Friedland had called and that we must all meet soon, Ajax and my mother didn't speak to each other but my mother's lover talked briskly to amuse my father. Afterwards when we went to the bar I contrived to pass Gennaro and whisper: "*Domani.*" He nodded. Leo and the other beachcombers didn't appear and we left early. It seemed we were all tired.

In the morning I was out early again but this time going the opposite way. The two strands on either side of Iticino spiaggia proper are called Molo d'Argento and Molo d'Oro, the natural one taken over by Leo and his friends being the silver one perhaps from the colour of the sand and the unnatural the golden perhaps hopefully since it's closest to where the fishing smacks are drawn up. The beach is heavy with black rocks and the local children fish and grub among them for sea treasures. Gennaro was already there perched uncomfortably on a dry rock and wearing light-grey flannels, shirt, and soft leather shoes while I was in shirt, shorts, and wooden *zoccoli*. He stood up and waved a little awkwardly as I scrambled towards him.

"*Ciao!*" I said.

"*Ciao.*" Gennaro put out his hand.

"You're very well dressed. Quite the gentleman."

He looked down at his legs and smoothed the neat knife-creased pants apologetically. "It seemed better to me."

"Why?" I was quite remorseless. "What can we do with you dressed like that?"

Gennaro laughed nervously again. "I can't stay long. I have to go soon. There are many things to do."

"A man of affairs." I resented the change in him very deeply.

He struggled to keep his dignity. "We are not children any more, Kit. It is not good for us to be together."

"What's the difference?"

We had first met when I was six. That year Fantah had come with us to look after me and we had gone, on our second day, in search of a beach where I could play while Fantah knitted one in the endless sequence of bright cardigans she wears over her sari. When English ladies no longer know what this woollen garment was it will be thought to be the exotic invention of Asian emigrants and the folk patterns, handed down for generations, ultimately derived from Sanskrit characters. The shoal of small boys who had fled at our approach had crept back to peer from behind rocks at her brownness, which was no more than their own, and my whiteness and at the fall of her long chiffon skirts. One, a little braver than the rest, came right out into the sunlight and stood staring.

"Little savages," Fantah said.

This one came quite close. "Kit," I said pointing to my chest.

"Gennaro," he answered stabbing at his own. It was a classic meeting. I looked around for the others but they had left the field. Without a common language we began to play together as children and lovers can. Every year after that we would meet. It was from Gennaro that I learned a lot of my Italian, though he learned only a word or two of English in exchange. At first we admired each other for our difference. Perhaps we were a little in love. Now we hadn't met for two years. Tokyo had intervened. He spread his hands in an imitated adult gesture.

" '*Scugnizz*,' " I said. I had always called him that,

after the city street urchins, and he had liked its faint suggestion of quick wickedness. "Or should it be young man now?"

"I have to go. My father . . . There's a lot of work. I go out with the boat and I make the accounts. It's a responsibility." He was both proud and frightened.

"And Renata?" He aped an adult grimace of knowing apology. "She's too old for you."

"One must begin and an older woman is good for a beginning," he said in stock answer. The old men had forced him up the next stage into the prearranged slot. "You will understand when you are older."

"We shall see." I had hoped to keep a precarious footing in a supposed childhood a little longer. Gennaro's defection might force me out too. I had expected more of the little boy who'd been first to come out of the shadow. He would be laughed at now if he was seen consorting with his juniors: the code was minutely defined and strictly kept.

"I have to go. I'm sorry." Then he added in English something he'd half heard at the movies and got me to teach him: "See you," and held out his hand.

"See you." We shook hands. I watched him go off towards the sea wall, pull himself up on it and walk along towards the village and the drawn-up boats with their strange high-beaked prows and barrel hulls painted as garishly as Chinese dragons. I wondered if he still knew what the phrase meant. I intended to take him at his word.

There was no discussion that day. When I got back my father and Ajax were replaying the tape, editing and typing from it. My mother was writing letters. Her correspondence is massive. She is on dozens of committees all over the world which she attends by mail and rarely in person, when, however, she drops a few hard diamond comments, enough to keep them happy for a year or so, and takes the next plane out. Her letters are incisive, often very funny and unmistakably hers, branded both by style and stationery.

I got a cold drink from the kitchen where the signora was already busy at the day's food, then I took a towel and went ostentatiously out through them all, across the small front garden, with its oleanders rose-flowered among tough sage-coloured slivers of foliage, swinging my towel, and turned left as if going down through the village to the sea but sharp left again and again til I was at the back wall of the signora's garden. A persimmon trailed its thin branches over the top. The stones of the wall were rough but the joining mortar, more sand than cement in the first place, crumbled into recesses that would give good toe-holds. The hill came down steeply cut into by the narrow lane I was standing in. It didn't seem to be overlooked; above was all scrub with a huge prickly pear like a watching triffid. But someone might come along; I would have to be quick. There was a door in the wall, locked somehow on the inside as I discovered when I tested it. I slipped out of my *zoccoli* and left them and the towel in a clump of weeds beside the door. The dust was very warm between my toes. I began to climb where the persimmon overhung, my bare flesh, knees, toes, and hands, shrinking from the abrasion of the gritty weathered stone. The first time I fell back unable to get a handhold anywhere, stubbing my toe and grazing my hands as I scrabbled. Then I got a toehold a couple of feet up, reached for some low branches that wouldn't hold me but kept my balance, drew up my free leg and pushed the foot into a crack so that I could thrust up and get an arm half over the top and draw myself onto it with the help of a stouter branch. I was gasping with fear and the effort as I looked back down into the lane. Nothing moved. Hidden from the house by the persimmon, I lowered myself from the wall and dropped into the garden.

There was the fig tree that had concealed Gennaro if indeed it had been he. How had he got in and out? He would have come calling in his best clothes and would have been unlikely to have scrambled over the wall in them by my route. The signora's was probably the best fenced plot in the village. Once again I looked about. There was no sign of the gardener. I examined the door. The catch which had seemed so solid on the outside was a piece of stick through two rusty hoops. Reaching in my shorts pocket I took out the knife I now carried as part of my inheritance from Jude and sawed halfway through the stick so it would snap under a sharp pull. There were plenty of other identical bits lying about the garden to replace it with. It was a chancy scheme but I couldn't think of any other. Someone might come along before I had a chance to use it, see the stick was split and replace it, but I had to risk that. There was always the wall if the door failed. I knew I could get in that way; I just didn't want to try it too often. Putting the piece of stick back through the hoops, I climbed the wall, easier on this side because of the tree, gave a quick look right and left, and dropped into the lane, landing with a plop and a spurt of dust. Towel and *zoccoli* retrieved I set off along the dirt track following it uphill. It plodded higher between hedges and occasional creeper-and-vine-swagged stone walls, sometimes intersected by other tracks which I took if they offered a more vertical way, marking where I'd turned off with tracking symbols. When I was seven I'd had a passion for lone scouting in one of my several favourite impersonations: the last of the Mohicans or one of the children of the New Forest. For the first time that knowledge was being put to a real use though it was true I had the miniature harbour and sea view below to guide me and now the Albergo del Golfo Azzurro, my goal above. Getting up there would take about ten minutes; coming back down would be much quicker.

The hotel was set down on a jut of rock as if a bird had put it there, a jut of rock padded with concrete and supported on slim columns. The balconies, one of which must belong to Ajax' room, looked towards the sea and below there was nothing but air for yards. I'd hoped to be able to overlook from a convenient tree but there wasn't a chance; nor could I climb those slender supports even when I knew which room I needed. Something else would have to be thought up. I turned back down the dirt lane following my markers accurately but bypassing our villa and keeping on down to the sea bearing towards the Molo d'Argento. This time I scrambled farther along the arm before I took my clothes off, hid them, and went swimming round the point. I was a bit tired after my full morning and it would soon be time to be back to the villa for lunch.

There was no sign of Leo as I got near in to the beach

nor of the somnolent logs of the other morning. He'd
kicked them into life and led them off somewhere. The
fire was quite dead and warm only from the sun. Apart
from that the beach seemed clean and litter free. Honeymoon Hotel was still there. I wondered if I would look
inside and then decided it was too risky. I didn't want to
be caught snooping. Still I didn't bother to swim back. My
body dried as I scaled the rocks and I put on my shirt tying
the ends in a knot across my belly and walked back
through the stares of the fishermen.

They were already eating when I got in. In our house
no one waits meals; it would seem an imposition as if you
were insisting that people should be back on time for the
sacred feeding ritual. "Had a good swim, darling?" my
mother smiled at me. Behind this she hid her concern that
I might drown while trying not to curtail my independ-
ence.

"Fine," I said. "I'm starving." The signora brought
me an outsized plate of pasta. She was smiling too and I
grinned back, playing the hungry and ingenuous child as I
sometimes do. It was *pasta asciuta:* big pieces of corru-
gated drainpipe in a strong sauce that I forked up into my
mouth and champed down with delight. The signora had
been making it when I left.

After lunch there was a movement towards the siesta
from my father.

"I'm the only one who hasn't seen your room yet," I
said to Ajax.

"Come up now if you like," my mother's lover
smiled.

"I might do that."

"You'd have to walk back."

I bit back the "It's not far" that threatened to leap out of my mouth like a freed soul at death in a medieval comic strip. It might have been all right. No one would have noticed but you had to begin somewhere being careful with words. They so easily give you away.

So I found myself climbing up to the Albergo again; this time by the paved road and in company. I laughed a little inside at the faint ache in my calf muscles. This time I went in through a white slit in the coffee fudge, across the marble floor to the blue and chrome desk where the receptionist sat reading a sci-fi paperback with little green men gamboling in red fields. *Il Microcosmo Verde.* Martian chatter in Italian seemed even more like Chipmunks.

"*Diciassette,*" said my mother's lover. "*Grazie.*"

"*Prego,*" accompanied the clatter of the key but his eyes were already straying back to infinity.

"Supposing they don't speak English?" I said as we went toward the lift.

"Who?"

"The little green men."

"I don't think they exist, do you?"

"No. It would be a comforting thought."

"That they do?"

"Yes." We shut ourselves in the little plastic coffin, to accommodate four persons only, and went up a floor.

"If they do," said my mother's lover, putting the key in the lock, "then we're not alone, we don't have total responsibility for the universe and that's comforting. However, one thing's certain: if they do exist they're technologically no further ahead than we are."

"Why?"

"Because since we're so close to getting there if they were more advanced than us they'd have been here by now."

I went to the window and looked through the shutter slats onto the balcony. "Perhaps they haven't the same curiosity."

"It's not curiosity; it's simple placing of empirical brick on brick, cause and effect. If that's a correct theory then it would apply to them too."

"You mean they wouldn't have any choice?"

"What do you think?"

The room smelled faintly of some perfume. I wondered if it was my mother's. Ajax came forward, opened the glass doors, then the shutters, and we walked out onto the balcony. It was a fine view to the sea and beyond. Among the foliage I caught a smear of the dirt track I'd followed that morning and marked it by a burst of honeysuckle in the hedge to tell me I could be seen at that point. The sea hurt my eyes with its brilliance as I strained after the distant shadows that might be the fishing boats putting out or simply lying off shore for the slaughter of innocents. We leaned on the rail for a moment with the sun beating us unmercifully so that my head sang.

"It's too hot for sight-seeing." Ajax led us back into the room, which though not cool was more dimly restful when one of the shutters was drawn to, the other left a little ajar.

It was a double room with twin beds and private bath. In fact there was double service in everything, wardrobes, dressing tables, in classic art deco light oak veneer with metal trimmings, padded quilted chairs and bed-heads.

"Have a bed." Ajax waved a hand at the one nearest the window. "I'd offer you a drink but I've only got scotch and I don't think you like that."

"No thanks. But you go ahead. I'd like some water if it's drinkable."

"It doesn't say it isn't and being a double room there are even twin glasses." My mother's lover went into the bathroom and there was the sound of running water. "I ran it as cold as I could but after a bit it doesn't come any colder."

"Thanks."

Ajax went to a dressing table, pulled open a drawer and took out a bottle of Johnny Walker Black Label, poured a third of a rich amber tumbler with precise movements, recorked the bottle and set it down on the glass top. The room was monastically bare apart from the indigenous furnishings and the scotch bottle and one pair of shoes standing neatly at attention beside the suitcase rack that held Ajax' case. There were no clothes flung over chairs, no books, no papers. At a glance through the door you might have said the room was uninhabited except for that faint lingering scent.

"Can I use your john?"

"Go ahead." Ajax had taken the other bed, leaning up on one elbow the better to tilt the glass. I went through into the bathroom and soundlessly bolted the door. It was a little less ascetic. Pants and socks hung drying over the rail of the shower curtain. A drip-dry shirt swung ghostly on a coathanger. I peed as silently as I could, hitting the porcelain side rather than the water. For someone to hear you peeing gives them power over you. Ajax had enough of that already. A plastic washbag drew my eye but it was too risky to try examining the contents. On the shelf above the basin was a yellow toothbrush that looked new and an almost full tube of English toothpaste, plastic white and very peppermint. I opened the door and called through.

"Can I borrow a towel? I'd like to wash my face a bit. It's still salty."

"Go ahead. There're plenty of clean ones."

I shut the door and splashed about in the basin. Then I dried on a clean facecloth, took the soiled one from its hook and put my nose to it trying to inhale the savour of my mother's lover. There was only a faint smell of soap. I swapped the two towels and opened the door. "Thanks."

Ajax smiled.

"You should say: 'You're welcome.' "

"The English don't have a polite equivalent. Is that because we don't mean it?"

"Could be."

"What do you think of yourself as?"

"World citizen number something or other."

"Have you got an American passport?"

"At the moment. But there are several others I could have if I wanted them. Do you swim?"

"A bit. I used to be quite good but you soon get out of practice."

"I swim every day."

"Perhaps I could join you sometime?"

"You do that." I was back on the bed, consciously relaxed, smiling across the gap as Ajax raised the glass. Tonight Ajax would wipe on the towel I'd used, hands, face who could tell, and unwittingly mingle our sweat for there is always sweat, oils and salts from the skin even after a wash, for the towel to take up. "I'd better be getting back." I swung my legs off the bed.

"See you at dinner."

"What's today?"

"Thursday I think. I'm beginning to lose account of time here already."

"We'll be eating out. It's the signora's night off. She doesn't like it but my father insists. We usually go to the pizzeria. I like it."

"Pizza?"

"Yes, but not like you get anywhere in the world north of Naples. See you." For the second time that day I went down the hill but running this time because suddenly I was tired.

My mother woke me. I had slept heavily and long. Ajax had come and they were ready to go but there was still no sign of me. I woke to her bending over my bed. "Kit, Kit, wake up, darling." Her perfume, heavy and musk, drowsed into my dreams. Or had it already been there?

"You're very beautiful," I murmured.

"Thank you, darling, but you must be still asleep." She drew the hair away from my eyes and kissed me. My mother has never stinted me of physical affection, having read all the right books and being herself of a mammalian warmbloodedness like that which caused small furry animals to huddle together for warmth or cats to doze in sun or firelight. It might have been thought that Sanskrit and shyness would make her less affectionate; it wasn't so. In these moments when she bent over me I was drugged by her very presence into a state of calm pleasure such as I only usually felt floating free in the warm salt water on my back with my eyes closed against the sun that let its effulgence flow over my limbs while an occasional small wave rocked me almost to sleep. "Is it the pizzeria?"

"Yes."

"I'll be down soon."

She got up and went out. It was almost dark, that quick twilight that black night so soon washes through in the South, not like the long Romantic summer dusks of Olde or New England or the nightlong dawns of Grandmotherland. I closed the shutters firmly and the windows against mosquitoes before switching on the light. The Iticino mosquitoes are peculiarly virulent. I have lain awake in the dark listening to the dive-bombing whine as they pitched towards naked and vulnerable flesh, sat up in frenzy, put on the light and swatted them into bloody blots on the wall—my blood. Next day swollen weals testified to their visit like the toothmarks of succubi, weals that could inflate a limb with the poison from those small rapiers deadly as Laertes' venomous foil. Their favourite spot was the eyelid, bringing it up as effectively as any prize fighter.

The pizzeria stood a little to the side of the main piazza. It was just a hut enclosing the oven where the *pizzaiuolo* worked, leading onto a walled courtyard roofed with an enormous vine. The tables and chairs were rickety but there was a clean paper cloth for every set of customers and the one white wine served was cold and dry. The pizze I had already praised to Ajax. They were also incredibly cheap which meant that everyone used the place. I liked it not only for the food and drink but for the chance to observe. When we got there it was already crowded; the *pizzaiuolo* in white chef's hat and apron was slapping the dough from a bun into a flat plate with rapid turning movements, sprinkling with oil, dotting pieces of cheese and tomato and thrusting the pancakes into the furnace belly of the oven so that his face was alternately puce and pallid as if he'd floured it with the pizza. Maybe his features were only stuck on: olives for eyes, a slice of tomato for the mouth, a Mozzarella nose with caper nostrils. We ate and drank with conversation made impossible by the noise. Coffee you took at one of the bars; those who'd just eaten together splitting for this refinement into Lilliput and Brobdingnag, though which was which I couldn't decide. Sometimes the fishermen seemed the giants and then under my cooling stare they would shrink to pinpoints as figures in dreams do.

So there we were in this bar as you might say barely settled in to our espressi and cognac when in comes Leo and some of his tribe except of course that we were outside and it was only because of a ripple across the way among the residents that I realized that they'd joined us. I'd been searching the faces for Gennaro but he was keeping away tonight.

"Some friends of mine," I said, jerking my head in the direction of the group, and getting to my feet. "I'll just have a word with them." My father nodded.

I crossed toward them between the tables and chairs. We always sat at the front where it was darkest; they took the table just outside the bar where the light fell thick for the guitarist to fret by or to ensure a deeper feeling of isolated community with the dark shutting them off. There were four of them including Leo: a pale Negro; a Jewish girl who would be called Gerry, Carole, or Sally Ann, and a wolfish boy in tattered denims who wouldn't say anything but would alternately sneer and look abstractly out to express his superiority.

"Hi!" I said to Leo.

"Hi." He looked up from tuning the guitar and down again, watching his hands with his head cocked like a Central Park squirrel, listening and adjusting the pegs. "Gerry, Jon, Okie—Kit." He nodded his head at the other three in turn. Okie nodded too. Gerry, I'd been right first time, said, "Hi," and Jon grinned. I smiled frankly all round.

"Where you from?" Gerry asked.

"Me? Everywhere."

"Good place to be from. They can't ask you for nothing," Okie said and shifted his gum back to a more central chewing point. I realized I had read him wrong.

"Okie's a draft dodger," Leo said, punctuating with plucked notes.

"Hey!" Okie said in protest.

"Oh, Kit's alright. Ain't you, Kit?"

"Yes, I'm alright. Good luck."

"You talk like a Limey. Jon's a Limey." Gerry smiled at him and he lowered his eyelids.

"A black Limey, how about that." Leo twanged.

"I come from nowhere and I'm going everywhere," Jon laughed.

"I saw you come around this morning," said Gerry.

"There didn't seem to be anyone about."

"We were in the hotel. I heard you and got up to look." She and Jon, I thought. I was very glad I'd been so cautious and not an obvious snooper.

"Where're all the rest?" I asked.

"We had a good clear-out this morning. Those who'd been here a bit wanted to move on down to Sicily. So I said, 'Get the hell out and leave me some peace.' So they did. Amateurs, college kids. Only these three left now."

"I'm no amateur, man. I'm running," said Okie.

"The Arkansas Traveller," and Leo played a few recognizable running bars. "You Okies always been dirt farmers. How come one of you started to think?"

"We always been on the move on account we always been poor. Your society ain't never given us nothing so why the hell should I fight for it. I just come a bit farther than most."

"T'aint my society, man."

"You've always got coloured people to fight each other for you," Jon said, smiling, to take the string out.

"That's what our black boys back home say. I'm on the side of anyone don't want to fight. I don't care if he's a blue-arsed Pawnee crossed with a billy goat."

"My guitar playing offend you, man?" Leo asked Jon. "See, he's a real musician. Writes the stuff," he explained.

"No one's music offends me if he wants to make it."

"Oh, I want to make it cos it makes me dread. Just now I'm resting but in a few weeks I'll hit it across to Rimini or maybe up to San Marino and shake up a few bucks playing to the real tourists not this screwball lot. That your old man? He looks expensive and a real tight-wad."

"That's him. Ask him for a dollar and he'll trade you for a footnote."

"He reminds me of my father," Gerry sighed. "Solid, respectable."

"Oh he's above all that."

"Gerry's the real amateur."

"Yeah, I guess that's true. I've run off for a couple of years but I know it's all waiting for me and I'll run back in the end. I depress myself. Home; it's a terrible word."

"Be happy," said Jon.

"I try, I do try."

"You work too hard at it."

"It's not natural to me. I've not been brought up to it."

"Smaltz!" Leo struck a loud discord.

"I guess it's hereditary at that." Gerry shook her head.

I got up. "I'd better get back. See you all around." They nodded and murmured. Leo began to play a coherent tune that resolved itself into "The Lily of the West." This time I walked back on the outside of the tables imagining the ripples of comment. Leo's voice sang out.

> "But she turned unto another man
> Which so oppressed my mind."

"You seem to know them quite well," said my father.

"That's Diogenes, only he's gathered a few disciples."

"Camp followers." My father laughed at his own joke.

"He thinks you look expensive."

"To buy, yes I am."

"And a tightwad."

"What did you say to that?"

"I could use some pocket money."

"I'm sorry, I forgot you usually get an allowance when we get here. I'll see about it tomorrow."

"Maybe we should include Diogenes in some of our discussions," I said and before anyone could protest: "I think you might find you were saying the same things."

"Why not," said Ajax and my mother nodded. It's difficult to provoke when your parents are so rational. A sudden chill such as comes sometimes off the sea after nightfall moved through the little piazza. My mother shivered.

"Are you cold? I'm afraid I haven't a jacket to offer you." My mother and her lover looked into each other's eyes and I saw the world fall away for them and heard the roaring in their ears. Were they already lovers? I had to know.

"Perhaps we should go," said my father. It seemed that Renata and the signora weren't appearing this evening.

It was a few days later that fate, as they say in other books, played into my hands and provided an answer to my problem. I had kept away from the Molo d'Argento, taking my morning swim from the main beach without rounding either of the points. Once Ajax came with me.

My mother's lover dropped shirt and pants beside my own little Crusoe heap and waded out to fling forward in a half dive and strike out in a tolerable though not exciting crawl. Far enough out my mother's lover flipped over and lay inert, slightly rolling in the water as if in a hammock, then with a fillip of the tail spurted away in a backstroke, turned over for a little underwater foray, came up, spluttered and moved off parallel with the shore in a slow but solid breaststroke. Ajax was the kind of lazy swimmer who might have once been good with a bit of exertion but now was just happily at home in the water. My mother's lover had the broad shoulders and powerful legs of the potential athlete with the golden hairs first wet dark then glinting as the sun dried them, and sanded with grains of salt. We lay face down on the beach for a little. By now I was beginning to be quite tanned but Ajax was still very white and concerned about not taking too much sun at first. A shadow fell across us, making me lift my head from the hot, shaded contemplation of salt and weed smelling beach between my bent elbows.

"Why, Kit, I thought it was you. How lovely to see you."

"Why, Ellie, how lovely to see you. Father told us you'd called. This is Ajax."

"How do you do." My mother's lover leapt up and shook hands like a perfect English gentleman, except that nowadays it's only elderly members of the working class who still do it, according to my father who is after all the social expert.

"I wonder if you'd just look after the children for a bit. I have to go and find one of the fishermen."

"Sure," I said, "but don't be long. We have to be back for lunch. You know what a stickler father is for precision." I could say this knowing that I was giving a totally false impression without telling other than the strictest truth. It pleased some artistic sense in me.

"Oh, I'm sure you'll both take very good care of them," Ellie said, giving my mother's lover one of her most defenceless and winning looks.

"They won't mind staying with us?" queried Ajax.

"Oh no, they're used to strangers and anyway Kit isn't strange. Truly I shan't be long. Be good kids now," and she was gone to the strains of Mimi.

"Of the second marriage," I muttered to Ajax. "How old are you now, Otto?"

"He's seven and I'm six," said Karen.

"That's right," said the boy. Obviously she was the boss.

"Well get on and play," I said.

"But not too far out," said Ajax.

"Come on," said Karen, "you're so slow," and led her brother off to a rocky outcrop with a convenient pool I remembered from my own brief childhood. I thought how much better the Molo d'Oro was for such activity but somehow I didn't want to take them there and covered my not wanting by saying to myself that their mother might come back soon and miss them.

"*Si dice* that he's named after Otto Schulzberg who was her conductor for a time and that it's really his child but I don't think even Ellie would be that thoughtless though it might be her only way of remembering who was, the father I mean."

"It breaks down when you come to the girls."

"Oh I don't know," I said and sank my face back into the marine gloom from which Ellie had raised it.

"I'd better put my shirt on before I get lobstered." Somehow I didn't want my mother's lover covered up yet. I found myself wondering how Ajax would look completely undressed and coming towards me. I wanted to fight, to wrestle, to hurt or be hurt. "Come on," I jumped up. "You can't get burnt if you're in the water," and I dashed into the sea. One of the great advantages of Iticino's main beach is the evenness of the seabed and its freedom from pebbles and sharp bits of shell that can cut an unwary foot as effectively as glass. Stomping through the shallows I threw up cut glass sprays of drops that glinted and rainbowed the seconds they hung in the air like chandeliers. The effort spent my energy as I knew it would and I fell back on the deeper water to sink gently, my hair floating weed, my limbs resistless, boneless as jellyfish. Ajax had followed sombrely, with a neat seal dive that clove the water without rupturing it.

"Must keep an eye on the kids," Ajax called across the clear waveless glass that lapped me round, warm and sticky as my own sweat.

They were crouched by the pool with that terrifying absorption I remembered, but could now only feel vicariously.

"They're fine." But Ajax turned towards the beach and by the time I reached it had towelled, put on the shirt, and wandered over to the two stooped figures. I was glad when Ellie came to collect them though she didn't bring her fisherman as I'd hoped.

"Tell your father you're all to come to dinner soon. You too, of course." She turned to Ajax. "I'll call." The sentences were delivered in breathless recitative. I almost heard the plagal cadence as she took the children, one by each hand, to lead them away.

"I wish to read you all something," my father said when we were next gathered round the tape recorder. " 'By revealing to us the absolute mechanism of all action, and so freeing us from the self-imposed and trammelling burden of moral responsibility, the scientific principle of Heredity has become, as it were, the warrant for the contemplative life.' Doesn't that in part sum up what we were saying the other day?"

"Doesn't it rather hinge on the meaning of 'the contemplative life'?" Ajax suggested.

"It's Wilde, isn't it?" said my mother.

"Yes to both," my father turned from one to the other. "We agreed that it wasn't science, I think, in the sense of the pursuit of knowledge, at least not infinitely."

"He probably meant life itself," said my mother. "That would be in keeping with much of his thought."

"It's rather a 'calm of mind, all passion spent' suggestion of a life. Life is rarely still long enough to be contemplated," Ajax objected. "One can't suppose he meant the religious contemplative; it must have been the aesthetic. In fact isn't one of the points about *The Picture of Dorian Gray* the permanence of art and the transitoriness of life?"

"I think he would have liked his life to be a kind of fluid work of art which one created of impressions and actions like brushstrokes or the images of poems," said my mother.

"But we are hindered all the time by mortality."

"Still, if the life has existed then it always exists. It's most human beings' art form."

"Does it exist any more than music on a page without anyone to play it?"

"There may come along someone who can read music in his head. One of the attractions of biography is the possible finding of a work of art life."

"And because it's finite, bounded by cradle and grave, it can make a whole, like an artifact," Ajax said. They had been building the conversation between them while my father and I listened as to an antiphony.

"What about the chain of heredity?" asked my father. "Parents and children all leading from each other like linked molecules?"

"Most children are so totally different from their parents," I put in to save anyone else the embarrassment, "that you rather wonder what the connection is except possibly in the physical taking after."

"And their lives on the whole will be very different," my father said with relief, "unless their society is one that tries to crush them all into the same Procrustean bed. Even then the inner quality of their lives will be very different one from the other. However, as Ajax says, lives are untidy and mortal; they may vanish, indeed most of them do, without trace. What then?"

"It's not original," I said, "but it's art, isn't it? The only thing that meets all the requirements."

"Can you explain?" said my father, not because he didn't know himself but because he wanted me to put it into words.

"Well, every work of art is an end in itself, a creation. It's inexhaustible. Mozart isn't superseded by Brahms. They coexist; not like knowledge, where the new outdates the old. We can get as much pleasure from beautiful or exciting shapes, say those Peruvian pots, as the people who made them, maybe more, and so will people in another thousand years' time."

"Good!" my father was pleased with my performance.

"The pleasure part is very important."

"Pleasure comes from a release of energy, doesn't it?" Ajax asked. "Which is the feeling of being carried away."

"I think so. It's a matter of how you work the release mechanism, that's all, and art is one of the major ways of doing it."

"The Katharsis of Aristotle," said my father.

"The calm after orgasm," said my mother looking directly at Ajax.

"Without that release we can't be happy."

"And happiness is still our pursuit?" my father asked. We all nodded.

"Yes, because whatever a man thinks he's pursuing he is, in disguise, pursuing his own pleasure."

"Suppose he doesn't like what he's doing?" I asked.

"Then either he'll stop or, if he goes on, that gives him the greater pleasure. He may tell himself he's doing the right thing but it's because it gives him pleasure to do what he thinks is right. Even if it's very painful it may simply be that it's satisfying his desire for pain and therefore once again giving him pleasure," Ajax answered again.

"So we may take it that no one living in reasonable

freedom does other than fundamentally what he wants to do. What are the exceptions to this?"

"External conditions make exceptions, like poverty, sickness, and limiting practical and social systems," my mother supplied out of her network of committees attempting to give everyone the same primary liberty she enjoyed herself. "They're problems that admit of a practical solution. But if you clear them out of the way, as we must do in time, then you can see the real problems of personality, of the understanding of the mind that can't be simply solved by technological progress."

"And we have come to a parallel with our last discussion," said my father as triumphantly as a conjurer producing the traditional white rabbit and he signed to Ajax to switch off the machine.

We were all somehow unwilling for the walk down to the piazza that evening. We lingered long after the signora's excellent dinner and Ajax drove away early. It was now accepted that my mother's lover had the car overnight for getting to the Albergo and back in the morning. My image of feet slapping down the dusty road and ploddingly up again at night had been driven out like all such charming rusticities by the advance of mechanization.

I think I must have fallen asleep but was suddenly wide awake listening with that hyperintensity that is only possible in the night. Yet I didn't feel I'd slept long. What had wakened me? I looked at the luminous green hands on my wrist. They lay together. It was only five minutes to eleven. My body throbbed with heat under the single sheet and my mouth was like the floor of a parrot's cage. Lulled by the heavy food I'd had more wine than usual this evening. I would get up for a drink. But I didn't switch on the light. I padded through the black cotton wool of the room towards the john door. Halfway across a sound stopped me. I changed direction for the window. It had been, I thought, a whisper, a human voice. I peered between the slats of the shutters but the glass made it difficult to see. Could I risk opening the windows? I must. Easing back the catch I began very gently to move first one casement then the other. The dry wood left the sill without any protest. The whispering was resumed unmistakeably this time. Pressing my forehead against one of the slats I peered down into the garden but for a while I couldn't see anything until my eyes accustomed themselves to pick out tree and bush shapes and the end wall slightly greyer against the black.

Then I heard the slight scuffling a little to my left. I moved to the right-hand shutter and stared sideways.

"*Ma senti . . .*"

"*Vatene, mosca, zanzaro!*" That was Renata's voice. Something moved below. It seemed suddenly a little lighter and I could see the pale oval of an upturned face and a suggestion of a human shape.

"*Renata, aspetta . . .*" it pleaded.

"*Mosca,*" said the girl's voice again. There was a sound that might have been an opening window. The figure below stretched up a hand in supplication. It was raised above the ground on something I couldn't make out but it might have been a chair or a box. The girl gave a slight laugh. There was an unidentifiable hissing noise and the figure below yelped and collapsed. I thought I heard the window shut. Groping for the rubber sandals I pushed my feet into them and crept down the stairs, through the kitchen to the back door, taking with me the small torch I always keep under my pillow. The door opened noiselessly. I went through into the garden and switched on the beam for a moment to pick out the heaped figure of Gennaro, his arms doubled over his head, his breath drawn in quick gasps to ward off sobs. I bent over him.

"It's Kit," I whispered. "What happened?"

"I'll kill her. She sprayed me like a mosquito," he managed to get out.

I pulled at his jacket. "Come into the kitchen. We can clean you up."

"No no. She's a witch like her mother."

"You can't go home like that. They'll laugh at you."
He groaned and staggered to his feet. Half pushing, half leading, I got him into the kitchen, closed the shutters, and put on the fortunately rather dim light the signora burnt there. I wanted to clean him up without anyone knowing and get him away. I wanted him in my debt.

"*Mamma mia*, what did she use?" His hair was powdered with a white sticky dew that reeked of chemicals. Either she had aimed carefully or luck had made her miss his eyes but they were weeping from the fumes and maybe a bit of rage and self-pity too. I ran some water in the sink and found a packet of detergent to whip up a lather strong enough to dissolve the lethal stuff.

"Be careful with the eyes," I said as I bent his head over the suds.

"Friend," he began but I silenced him with a scoop of froth and he obediently screwed his fists into his swimming eyeballs. Whatever she'd used I wasn't able to wash away completely. Under the foamy assault it became a clinging dust but it was better than in its first state. I towelled Gennaro's head hard but the granules stuck to the roots like lice. However, by combing his hair carefully the top layer could be made to hide the rest. I showed Gennaro himself in the glass. With care no one need know. Then I put out the lights and led the way into the garden with my torch. He picked up the plinth he had been standing on when the goddess's scorn overtook him. It was a fishbox. When we came to the wall I saw a rope ladder hanging down on the inside, like the ratlines of a clipper, made from twisted net twine and ending in a grappling hook over the top of the wall. Gennaro flung his arms around me, and went up the ladder like a monkey or a midshipman, carrying the box in one hand. For a moment he perched on the top of the wall, then the ladder was drawn up and I heard first the box, then the ladder and finally Gennaro land on the other side. Keeping the accounts hadn't yet made him less nimble but then he'd said something about going out with his father too. Even in this seemingly passive sea fishing was hard work and sudden storms leapt up from a hand-sized cloud wanting their ritual appeasement of men and boats. I went back into the house.

With the shutters closed again I stood in the dark room feeling the house around me listening. Suddenly there was a click and light fell over me like a shower. My mother stood in the doorway, her hand still on the switch.

"Darling, whatever . . . ?"

"I was hungry." I pulled open the icebox door.

"Why in the dark?" She came forward into the room.

"I was looking into the garden. It's very beautiful. I thought I heard something."

She nodded. "You won't be long will you, darling?"

"No, no." I took a cold wing of chicken from a plate and put it between my teeth though I wasn't hungry. Why was she up? Maybe she'd been out. She had a light coat on held together over what? As if she guessed my attempts to undress her she moved toward the door.

"Was there anything?"

"Where?"

"In the garden."

"Oh yes. No, only the trees. I thought it might be someone for the signora."

"Yes it might have been." And she was gone. I heard only the faintest of creaks as she went up the stairs. Stockings and shoes, those were the things I should have looked at and for and I'd missed. I put out the light and took the half-eaten limb up to my room, disgusted with my failure. As I stepped across the threshold I remembered the open window. The mosquitoes would be in in their thousands. I crossed, opened the shutters, and hurled the piece of cold dead bird in mock flight as far as I could. In the morning my left shoulder was ridged with small red hills as if a Lilliputian mole had been at work under the skin. It seemed time to give Leo another visit. Besides I'd always believed in the therapeutic value of the bathe both from experience, perhaps beginning with the pleasures of bath time with Fantah, and with the sanction of its long history.

However, as the shore moved towards me, as it appears to do rather than the swimmer moving in his immensity of ocean, I saw that once again it was empty. Still I kept on till I was close in enough to wade when the motion became mine. There might be someone in Honeymoon Hotel again who could see me and wonder why I had turned back. As the last wave rippled away from my feet a canvas flap was lifted and Gerry came toward me.

"Hi!"

"Hi!"

I've often thought about this meaningless interjection. Is it a contraction of "Howdy" or "Hail" or the Indian "How"? I see no purpose in it. At St. Gelbert's I soon moved to the more formal salutation but I'm aware of the value of the friendly hiccup in certain situtations. So we hiccuped at each other.

"Where's everybody?"

"Leo took them off for the day."

"You didn't want to go along?"

"I got the feeling they wanted a stag party."

I spread myself out to dry in what I hoped was an engaging and frank way. She wasn't exactly pretty: her skin was too coarse and her nose not any shape but her hair was long, dark, and curly and her eyes a deep blue. She had a conventionally good figure but she would be hairy when she was older. Already the skin was shadowed by a fine black down.

"Must be pretty hot in there." I nodded towards the canvas shack.

"Yeah but it's private. Oh God I'm so sick."

I murmured sympathetically and looked encouragement. Gerry crouched down beside me and dug about in the sand with a waterice stick.

"I want to talk to someone but I know I shouldn't and anyway you're still a kid. How do you stand this heat?"

The cliff behind tumbled towards us in the sunshimmer while the silver beach danced up to meet it, as undulating as Salome, until I felt myself drowning in light waves more tangible than the salt ones I'd just left. "I find it sorta psychedelic but I guess I'm high enough at that. Let's go over to the shade." I pointed to the rocky, seal-black overhang of the spur. "I'm not that young," I said when we were out of the sun's throb. " 'I been people and seen places' as the lady said. Anyway, some people are born old. I'm one of them."

"I guess ages don't matter." She took off her sandals and dabbled her feet in the water. The sandals were thonged with tooled and gilt patterns, too delicate for the rough craftsmen and rocks of Iticino. They were beginning to fade and tear under their harsh usage. "Maybe in world time you're older than me. Maybe last time you were the guru and I was the disciple."

"Or you were the stone and I was the limpet."

"I don't know whether I buy that; that's transmigration."

"I'm not sure I do but supposing the balance of elements is constant in the earth with its atmosphere, then the carbon and nitrogen cycles would mean something very close to it. They're all just trying to make sense of experience, all the systems."

"You're pretty smart."

"Out of the mouths of babes . . ." I threw a pebble plop into the water.

"Don't give me that Christian crap."

"It's no worse than any other except it's more familiar."

"Maybe you're too smart."

I'd overshot myself. I'd have to retrench a bit to get her confidence. "I can't help it. It's my parents. They're very smart. They talk about everything. I've got nothing to protest over."

"It doesn't always work out like that. Mine're smart too but they're so entrenched we just can't talk and my mother's so emotionally grasping."

I threw another pebble and she looked round the little bay and sighed. "Me and Jon had a fight. I'm just so sick I don't know if I'll ever be whole. When I came to Europe the freedom so hit me I think I went out of my mind for a bit. I'm a very unstable person. I went to school and college and did all the right things but inside I was just flying apart and hating it all and hating me. So I lit out and came here. I'm learning all the time but it's hard and long and I don't know if I'll ever make it."

"It's always terrible at first. All the attitudes you've been brought up with get stood on their heads. Everyone goes a bit crazy."

"Jon's a very lovely person. He's real. He's not like me. I'm a shit. You know something: we're so mixed up with race back home we overcompensate."

"I know. American girls in Europe first thing they do is get themselves a coloured boy, any colour, because they're so guilty."

"I know, I know that's what I've done and I'm a shit. I don't love Jon; I just want to love him. And he's worth more than that. Jesus what a mess."

"He's probably used to it," I hit her hard.

"I've unloaded all my guilt on him and now I'm twice as guilty. I just feel ill all the time."

"You want to get away and look at it in perspective."

"Another terrible thing: I hate this beach and this crummy way of life. I'm so conditioned like everyone back home to being clean and comfortable my whole self just revolts at the squalor and yet I know that's just bourgeois and materialist. The real guru is so beautiful inside that even when he's lousy and filthy and covered with sores he smells of lotus blossom. Me I just stink."

"Like I say," I said evenly, "you need a change for a while that's all. Your system's had a deep shock. You need to contemplate for a bit."

"Meditate you mean?"

"That's right. Read a little. Clear your mind."

"Oh how I want a bath. I want to steep myself and lather myself with scented soap and blow bubbles like a kid and then steep myself some more."

"You want to be all clean inside and out."

"You're so right. That's just it; somehow purified and at peace."

"Why don't you move into a hotel for a few days."

"Oh my God if I could."

"Why not?"

"First I'd feel like I was opting out. Second I can't really afford it. I've got some money my grandmother left me that I used to come over but I have to make it last."

"The first is emotional not rational and if you think about it you'll see I'm right. The second I could help with."

"You?"

"Oh strictly for my own reasons."

"I don't get it."

"Let's say I want the occasional use of a room in a hotel."

"You hooked?"

"I like a smoke from time to time," I lied. "I can't do it at home."

"Your parents aren't that liberal?"

"They'd say, 'Of course darling if you must,' and worry themselves sick."

"I know the whole syndrome."

"I've got plenty of money. It's worth it to me."

"Why can't you just get a place yourself or go away somewhere for a quiet smoke?"

"There's nowhere quiet except here," I looked round the beach, "and I don't want to get too involved. Everywhere else there're always people wandering about and you know how the stuff smells. I can't get a room myself because for one you have to have a passport and my old man'd want to know why I needed mine and I'm too well known here anyway. But I could visit a friend. We could have some arrangement, a towel hung over the balcony if you'd got company or didn't want me in. I wouldn't want it all that often and I'd go halves on the rent. When you're sick of it we call it quits."

"It'd be nice." I could see her wavering. "But you're a minor. I hate to think what the law says."

"But then we don't run our lives by the laws."

"It'd give me a reason to make it easier with Jon. He knows I'm sick. It'd be so nice to sleep in a real bed."

"And that bath!"

"When shall we do it?"

"Why wait? I'll get my clothes while you get your things."

By the time I'd climbed over the spur, dressed, and come back Gerry was standing beside a suitcase and a big embroidered Hessian bag. A camera, strap of books, a handbag, and a plastic carrier sprouted around her feet. I picked up the suitcase. "Let's go before they come back. It's easier to negotiate from a position of strength." I took her the back way along the dusty lanes since the main route led past our villa. I didn't want to be seen with her yet.

The sweat poured off us as we carried her gear uphill. In the track below the jutting balconies we paused for Gerry to comb her hair and mop the pale, damp features.

"I'll do the talking if you like," I offered.

"Thanks. I don't have much Italian." I'd guessed it would be so. I asked for a room with private bath and balcony for my friend, hoping the receptionist hadn't seen her in bad company but if he had he didn't recognize her in mine. With luck he'd think she'd just arrived on a visit. "Sixteen, seventeen, and eighteen are beautiful rooms," I smiled at the receptionist.

"Sì, sì, bellissime." He turned to the board and then put a key marked eighteen on the desk. "And the young lady's passport?"

Gerry handed him the hostage and we were in. My

thighs trembled with excitement as we stopped at the door beyond Ajax'.

"What will you do first?" I asked when we were inside.

"Take a bath. Will you look at it—all cool and white. Isn't that the most inviting sight ever?"

"Can I use your john before you rush in?"

"Go ahead. Half of it's yours."

Once inside and the bolt across I climbed on the seat so that I could reach the ventilator, took my knife from my pocket and levered out the four small screws at the corners of the grating. They came out as easily as I'd hoped they would. I put the grating carefully on the top of the cistern and reached my hand into the hole until my fingers came up against Ajax' companion grill. Then I took a piece of twine from my pocket, threaded it through one bar and back and began to gently prise the grill outwards. It yielded easily from the soft plaster. I turned the oblong sideways and drew it back towards me. Chest tight and heaving, I peered through the gap. The bathroom door was open and I could see into number seventeen, though it was only a limited view that could be cut off by the closing of that door. Ajax' grill I stood diagonally in the small passage and replaced the other on the outside. If my mother's lover noticed the lack of a cover and stood on the seat to look through there would be nothing but a dark cul de sac that would allay all suspicion. My knife and the piece of twine safely back in my pocket I flushed decisively and went back to Gerry.

"I thought you'd died in there." She'd probably decided I was on the hard stuff and had been shooting up.

"Sorry, I got to thinking. What about the signal?"

"I reckon the towel as you said. Right now I'm going to take me that bath. Cleopatra won't have nothing on me. Then maybe I'll go down and break it to Jon. Suppose you want to come when I'm not here?"

"I'll deal with that. If I see the towel I'll take it you're busy and not come. There's just one thing." Gerry looked a question. "Sometimes I may need to come quite late. You can't tell when it'll take you so if you always make sure about the towel."

"You mean only put it out when I'm in bed with someone."

"That's it."

"Jesus, you're desperate. No wonder you needed a room."

On the way down I smiled and greeted the receptionist. This time I took the risk of the main road. I'd have to get a bit of pot to burn for the sake of the smell and after lunch I'd go shopping. At table I chattered and quipped with my mother's lover until my mother looked at me rather anxiously. My frantic high spirits were worrying her.

In the afternoon I bought two square purse mirrors such as Italian women still carry with them, white cardboard, plastic sealing tape, and strong glue, which I carried up to my room where I spent a happy couple of hours as if I were a child again building the kind of periscope people use for watching processions, royal progresses, over the heads of the route-lining crowds, to observe my own royal or divine tableau. Somehow I felt sure both my mother and Ajax would think that to close the bathroom door was to pander to the tasteful proprieties of mag-and-ad sex. My toy completed I slept the dreamless sleep of innocence. When I woke I went out into the garden, undid the stick bolt of the gate, and went into the lane. It took me only a short search to find Gennaro's box and ladder hidden behind a clump of azalea.

Leo and Okie came alone into the bar that evening. I imagined the towel discreetly hanging over the balcony.

"Aren't you going over to see your friends?" my father asked. I got up and sauntered across.

"Have a nice trip?" I grinned at Leo. He smiled gently and I looked deep down into his eyes. They were deep enough to drown in.

"We took us into Naples for the day. Hitched. Got a good friend in that Jezebel city. Knows everyone comes into that port. Right now I feel kindly towards the world."

"I could use some stuff," I jigged a little to show my need.

"You got to have the bread if you want something to put it on."

"That's alright. I can take care of that. I'll come round tomorrow."

"You do that. If me and Okie haven't set the world to rights and burned ourselves all up."

"Don't do that. Save a piece of it for me."

"We'll try to think of you, man, won't we, Okie?"

"Sure, kid, we'll think of you."

They were both off flying somewhere out to sea. If I jumped hard and high enough I might catch their heel as they passed overhead. When I got back to the table Renata and her mother had joined us.

"Renata says tomorrow is a big fiesta," said my father.

"Yes, oh yes. Santa Venere delle Galline. It is to bless the boats. It is every year."

We had never been in Iticino so early in the summer before so we had never seen it but I had heard of this pagan benediction from Gennaro.

Leo hadn't forgotten me it seemed. I bought a small joint from him for only twice what he'd paid for it, half an ounce of coarse tobacco I reckoned was probably naval plug and even some papers.

"There's no need to tell anyone," I said. He would think I meant my parents but it was really Gerry I had in mind though it wouldn't have been disastrous if she'd found out my source was Leo.

"Shit no," he said. "I started to smoke in high school. I'm no blabbermouth. Anyone of intelligence has to have some counter to their terrible world, some way into coloured dreams out of their grey. Those old bastards made this deathly universe so they shouldn't wonder when kids go on pot as the only escape. They have their alcohol or they couldn't face it themselves. Your parents drink much?"

"Enough."

He nodded. "You see."

At lunchtime my father came in laughing and rubbing his hands. It was clear that he was waiting for someone to ask why so I obliged. I wanted everyone in a good humour.

"It's Renata. I went into the kitchen just now and what do you think she was reading?"

"*Tom Sawyer*," I said. His face fell. I could have

kicked myself but the moment of pleasure had been irresistible.

"I said I thought she was a little old for that. I suggested she try either something older and more adult like Jane Austen or something modern like Hemingway."

"He's certainly simple."

"I wasn't suggesting him as a great author, darling, just as a simple adult text."

"Technically I suppose one would have to call him that," my mother allowed grudgingly.

"Anyway I said I'd help her get started with it after lunch."

"Perhaps you'd like a drive?" Ajax turned to my mother.

"That would be nice. Kit?"

"I'm sleepy. I don't think I'll come." I lifted up a guileless face in which the eyelids were already beginning to droop towards her.

I gave them five minutes after the sound of the car had died away. My father's voice droned faintly from the kitchen as I crept down the stairs and went out into the front, ducked below window level and round into the back lane carrying my equipment in a bright plastic bag with books on top to make it look bulkier. I climbed quickly, sweatily in the afternoon sun, picking out my markers with a practised eye although I knew the route by now. At the honeysuckle I paused, wiped the stinging trickles out of my eyes, and looked up at the Albergo. The balconies were clearly visible from here. There was no towel. I left the lane for the open front, passing our car parked in the driveway, and ran quickly into the entrance hall.

"*Diciotto, per favore.*"

"The young lady has gone out."

"I know. She asked me to bring these back for her."

"I understand." He put down the key. I thanked someone, maybe Santa Venere delle Galline, that Iticino is small and easygoing. Besides he was eager to get back to Mars or was it Venus today, benevolent planet? And what harm could a child do, a dear young friend. The lift was too risky. I ran up the stairs and looked round the corner. The corridor was empty. Silently I reached the door, turned the key, and was inside with the now familiar choking tightness in my chest. Locking the door behind me, I emptied the bag at once onto the bed. I lit the half cigarette I'd rolled and cut earlier, drew a couple of deep breaths that I let flow out from my pursed lips without inhaling, and left the end to burn on the ashtray. Inside the bathroom now with its door locked lest the smell should drift through the open vent into number seventeen I went through my previous procedure with the skill of a cat burglar or Tarzan himself. As soon as I removed the grill I heard voices. Looking through I saw that the door was open as I'd forecast but it gave no view of my quarry. Silently I inserted the periscope in the tunnel. "Look here on this picture."

It was so perfect, my true still life, that I felt I had composed it. In a sense I had. Hadn't I isolated and framed it in the little reflective square of glass; made a double image of it so that for that brief time there were two copies and now there is only one hung everlastingly and secretly in my mind where no one else will ever see it?

Even the richest magnate has a tangible object which others may happen upon, inquisitive fingers pull the cord that draws the velvet curtains and see her smiling, fallen back in attitudes of desire or satiation, but no one now can ever stumble Actaeon upon my scene. I was myself the tracker of luminous game as if behind the wouldbe huntsman (for what else is a lover?) lurked another shadowy pursuer. Ajax stood in that taut stance I had first noticed in the pool of sunlight on the purple carpet before my mother who lay back against the heaped pillows of both beds. Because of the angled glasses the composition even had the foreshortening beloved of Renaissance painters. It might have been an annunciation.

"What is it?" Ajax said.

And my mother replied, "We have fallen in love; our imaginations have entangled."

I felt that I might be sick with excitement and found I'd been holding my breath. Somehow it seemed too risky to go on with at that moment. Withdrawing the periscope I put the two grills back and sank down on the cold edge of the bath shaking and running with sweat. Whether I had unwittingly inhaled some of the cigarette or whether it was the effect of the mirror or whether my eyes being glued to an area their own width, the image filled my whole vision I can't decide, but my head sang with shapes and colours, the contours of that landscape they had lit and walked in and planted my imagination with.

There was a butt end left in the ashtray which I took up for future use like any real addict. The room was convincingly heavy with "the fume of poppies." I put my periscope at the back of a bottom drawer in the unused dressing table together with a couple of the books and went downstairs with the plastic bag folded under my arm. Calling out a cheerful *"ciao"* I tossed the key down in front of the receptionist who hadn't noticed how long I'd been and ran quickly for the safety of the lane. Going down I tore off a sprig of honeysuckle and stuck it behind my ear not caring how bizarre it looked. I was the aboriginal flower child. The sounds coming up from the streets below I thought were louder than usual already, more carnival. As I had managed to get out so I got in again unobserved.

"Shall we go to the fair then?" asked my father after dinner, making it sound like a Massachusetts pig bowling, or an English guess-the-weight-of-the-marrow on the vicarage lawn. Already the narrow streets were crowded with families going down in lines abreast arms linked by sexes; the little piazza was lined with stalls selling nougat and slices of coconut and melon. Renata and her mother brought up the rear of our party, their high-heeled mules striking firmly in step on the cobbles. Fairy lights were laced round the square and led away down the main street to the beach. The two bars were packed and seething with movement and expectancy. A platform had been set up at one side where a brass band, mercifully muted, played selections from Verdi and Puccini, interspersed with Neapolitan folk songs beloved of Italian tenors and the most famous local pop songs.

"It's a very strange name," my father said when we were seated at a table the waiter had cleared and chaired for us as regular customers.

"St. Venus?" my mother asked, "or the chickens?"

"Both."

"There's a St. Venus of the Port farther down the coast," Ajax offered. "I saw it on the map when I was looking for something else."

"Soon," said Renata, "they will bring the madonna from the church."

"That's interesting," said my mother, "so someone's admitting that the madonna and Venus are the same."

"Only Venus was here first," I said.

"Yes, she was all down this coast. In fact I've seen it suggested that goddess worship was here before gods. Certainly many of the names of the goddesses got transferred to the madonna. It was conscious policy with the early church to rededicate all the local cults and shrines to saints if they were to a god or hero and, as I've said, to her, if they were to a goddess or nymph."

"But all the goddesses are only attributes or facets of the one whatever name you call her by, aren't they?" my mother's lover asked.

"You may be right," she laughed back. "But what about the gods?"

"I don't think the same applies. They may be father god or they may be siblings or they may be lovers of the goddess or even ego ideals—heroes."

"But only one goddess?" she teased.

"Yes, only one entire and perfect chrysolite."

"What does the madonna do?" my father asked Renata.

"She blesses the sea. She makes the fishes come."

"And baby," said the signora unexpectedly.

Renata smiled her controlled cool smile. "My mother

thinks these people barbarians but it is good for her business."

"The seaborn Aphrodite of fecundity; it all fits together," said my mother. Out of the corner of my eye I saw Gennaro for a moment as the restlessly shifting swell of walkers parted. He grinned and pointed to his hair and gave the thumbs-up sign he'd learned from the movies.

"She is coming," said Renata and pointed down that street to the sea which held the church. A knot of people approaching in the dark resolved itself into a procession that advanced on the square. The band stopped; there was a moment's breathheld silence and then we could hear the harsh chanting of boys interspersed with the fuller tones of the priest. First came acolytes with a big flat silken, banner behind a thurifer who swung his cloudy censer to left and right, then the priest supported by more boys, the statue borne on a litter by four strong fishermen, local dignitaries, the fishermen's leaders with another banner, and then small boys darting among them like sardines, the rest of the village joining in as they were passed, the men crossing themselves, the women genuflecting. The procession visited each side of the square in turn, the priest casting holy water and blessings, the statue bowing in benediction through the kind offices of her bearers.

For it was the statue that drew us all. She was very old and ugly. Her painted wooden face stared unmercifully, uncomprehendingly over our heads, undinted by our offerings of faith and obeisance. Her wooden arms were flung out stiff as crosstrees. But what was most strange was that she was dressed over-all in a shawl of feathers, living feathers that moved and clucked, feathers of all colours that clung to her shoulders and perched along her arms and clustered at her feet, and on her head a pure white bird like a tiara, Diana's moon, Athena's owl. I wondered if they were drugged to keep them there. We had all risen. My father put down some money on the table and drawn like the rest we followed the procession out of the square and back down the street towards the sea. From time to time women ran forward to put money in the silver salver carried by one of the robed boys and to cross themselves curtseying and muttering to that unmoved face.

We reached the end of the village and set off across the beach. The fishing boats were all lit. Lanterns marked the route along the concrete mole. Each boat was blessed in turn, the chanting rising in the dark air thin across the black water. I pressed forward. I heard my mother calling me but I kept on, wriggling through the crowd. The priest had dropped back but the litter bearers went on towards the end of the pier. The crowd too had stopped but was looking after the statue followed only now by the dark jerseyed fishermen. Suddenly I found Gennaro at my side. "What is it; what are they doing?"

"The white cock," he said.

There was a pause. We all waited. Then they were coming back. The crowd shifted a little. Now we could see Santa Venere rising out of the dark foam of night. Her white diadem had gone but a kind of excitement moved through the crowd. I felt it move in me. People began to chatter and laugh as we went up the hill. The statue with its official attendants passed through the door into its shrine. I fought my way back to our group. My father stood tall and broad, unmistakable above the smaller inhabitants.

"Well," he was saying, "After that a drink I think."

"There you are," said my mother.

"*Sta ammazzad!*" I chopped the air with the side of my hand.

"Several drinks." My mother shivered.

The band was playing again. My father ordered cognacs all round. Laughter and talk rose about us. Soon Leo and the others took up their usual table and began to compete on guitar with the band, who anyway had finished their paid efforts in a little while and disappeared. Ajax bought us all more drinks. A curious lighthearted (or was it headed)-ness took hold of me. My mother and her lover were smiling at each other. The signora nodded contentedly. My father and Renata played their cool checkers.

"Signora, signora!" A man stood by the table, one of the fishermen by his hands and dress. "*Mia moglie!*"

The signora got up at once. Renata and she exchanged a few quick words. She smiled and said goodnight to us and followed the man out of the piazza towards the villa, where she would collect her bag.

"Perhaps we should go too," said my mother. "You must be tired, darling." Slowly we climbed the hill. I said goodnight and went upstairs. On the landing I waited by the window. Very shortly my mother and Ajax appeared as faintly luminous shapes below. I heard the car start. Then I crept down the stairs into the kitchen. My father's and Renata's voices came from the other room. I closed the kitchen window but left it unfastened and then went through the front door into the cover of the night. With Gennaro's ladder about my body outside my shirt I worked quickly along my route, occasionally flicking on my torch. A little wind moved the foliage. A shape loomed suddenly but it was only a tall cactus I'd forgotten from daytime. As I climbed, my chest began its familiar choking clench so that at the honeysuckle I had to stop and gasp in the sweet air. Gerry must be still down in the bar. Was that a light behind Ajax' shutters? I counted balconies.

Avoiding the light spilling out of the hotel entrance I got to the side between the thin columns. The first time I threw up the grappling hook it fell back without touching the balcony, straight down like a tennis ball tossed for service. I managed to catch it before it clanged to the ground, paused a minute, feeling a feather tickle of damp blow over my body, and threw again, wishing for Gennaro's expertise. It caught with, to my ears, a huge clatter but although I waited, counting under my breath for two minutes, quite still, no one appeared. I'd been supremely lucky. Only the cognac had given me strength and courage to get the hook over the balcony at all I was quite sure. I tested it with a strong pull but I was sure Gennaro would have made it able to take more than his weight and I was even lighter. I managed to haul myself up to the bottom rung and then I was up and over the top, drawing the ladder up behind me. The catch of the French door I opened with my penknife. I was inside at last.

There wasn't any reason that I could see for not putting on the light. As I'd climbed I'd been aware of a faint radiance through Ajax' shutters like a distant galaxy you haven't time to examine. When the room was lit I practised deep breathing to steady myself and as soon as my hands no longer trembled I took out the periscope and went into the bathroom.

Ajax I couldn't see at first but my mother lay quite naked on the bed in my vision. I had often seen her naked before, since my father like most Scandinavians believes in family exposure, in the naturalness of nudity. He is quite wrong. There's nothing natural about a naked human being. Millennia ago in our civilised and artificial way we assumed clothing and our own covering moulted away. An animal is never naked. Even the pig and the elephant are hidebound, camouflaged, bristled. Man wears clothes as naturally as he speaks so that as a superlatively artificial and artful act he can take them off and catch the breath with his vulnerable beauty that painters have always perceived. Flesh is made not by God but by man and enhanced by beautiful gestures and attitudes into the art of love. I can say this now; I have seen it. My mother lay on the damask quilt in the dark, like that precious stone the alchemists prized, with the soft green and yellow fire from the black tarry heart of a nugget of coal. I had seen her walking about and admired in a domestic way the flow of limbs, the polished penetrability of skin, without understanding. This was quite different. Now as if I had shaken a kaleidoscope Ajax moved into the picture so that it became unfallen Adam and Eve, Eros and Psyche. My mother lifted her arms and her lover went into them to be entwined there. I saw the strong tensing of carved marble muscles as the knee thrust to part her thighs.

My attention was snatched back. The outer door had been opened. It must be Gerry. Salt blinded me for a moment but I didn't know if it was sweat or tears. I took out the periscope and put back the grill. I must get out before she called my name. Fixing my smile, I pulled the closet handle and opened the door.

"I thought you were here," Gerry said. "I knew I hadn't forgotten the light. What's that thing?" Then as a soft fierce crying broke after me into the room through the thin public walls, "Jesus, someone's enjoying themselves."

"It's something I'm making," I answered and shut the door.

"You're a strange kid. In there?"

"I do a lot of thinking in the john."

"And that?" she pointed to the rope ladder.

"I was afraid they wouldn't let me in so I climbed over the balcony."

"There's only a kid asleep down there. Everyone else has gone to the fiesta."

"I'd better go." I picked up the ladder.

"Have this." Gerry gave me a piece of *The New York Times*. "Jon brought it back from Naples. They see you with a ladder they'll get you for housebreaking."

"Thanks." For the second time that day I ran down the stairs. There was only a child asleep in a chair in the hall. I was out in the dark going downhill but my legs ached and threatened to drop me in the lane. I forced my-self on, put back the ladder with the box and almost too weak to push leaned against the garden door. The twigbolt snapped. With my torch I found another. The kitchen window was mercifully easy. I crept upstairs. The floor was a desert-vast tilting plain between me and the bed. I crossed it painfully, taking blurred light years before I could sink down. I must have fallen asleep at once for I woke some time later (had the car come and gone?), the periscope held to me. I undressed and slept again, stumbling and crying through my dreams as I fled after some impossible and indecipherable game.

I woke late. When I went into the kitchen only the signora was there. "Where are the others?" I asked, sipping the warm, milky coffee.

"Your father has gone to buy something—pencils I think. The others are in the garden."

"Thanks." I put down the empty cup and went through the back door. My legs still ached. The heat and light hit me a great enveloping blow so that I almost staggered. Then I caught a flicker of movement behind the signora's fig tree. I went forward silent on rubber sandals but not so that anyone could accuse me of creeping. This side of the large flat-leaved bush I paused.

"The Eve of St. Venus." That was Ajax' voice.

" '*Cras amet qui nunquam amavit,*' " chanted my mother.

" '*Quique amavit cras amet,*' " her lover answered her.

But the day was too hot and the sky wouldn't stay in place. It began to fall slowly towards me in a huge molten sheet like the lid of a giant silver chafing dish. Then I was lying on the burning plate of the ground like breakfast kidneys in my own seething juice, my mother and Ajax peering anxiously in at me as the lid came down.

~ Part Two ~

"He never happy lived
That cannot love to die."

John Dowland

SIGNORA GAMBARDELLA'S ASSISTANT, the doctor, pronounced it sunstroke, heat prostration, and exhaustion. The Italians still believe very seriously in "the nerves." No doubt he included them in his diagnosis. As soon as I was recovered enough my mother flew with me to Grand'-mère's. It was felt that the rest and the brisk bright northern summer would convalesce me. Disguising my fury was one of my better performances but my father had been taken by one of those firm decisions that I know are unshakeable. My parents were puzzled; my mother deeply worried by the strange suddenness of my collapse. It was true I felt very tired. I wrote to Gerry, sending her money and begging her not to leave before I got back. I nearly put: "I must to England; you know that," at the beginning of my letter but I was afraid she'd take me literally. Then I toyed a bit with: "He that is mad and sent into England," but that would have confused her too so I stuck to simple communication. I asked the signora to post the letter for me. I was to stay three weeks. At first it had been a month but I'd pleaded to the point of weeping so that my mother was afraid I'd make myself ill again as I knew she would be, and intervened for me.

Life with Grand'mère goes at sleighpace with a tinkle of bells and the cheerful trotting of deer. It's the Never

Never Land of perpetual childhood like the long summer day that quarries away night and black fears. I had time to read. Lying awake in the everlasting twilight I reread my *Myths and Legends of Many Lands*. Maybe I'd been wrong to concentrate so much on Venus to the neglect of Jupiter. But no. Jove loved lightly and not too well. I'd seen them all come and go. There was nothing remarkable there except that it wouldn't do not to know at all what was happening. The occasional sideglance should be enough to keep me up to date. I felt myself at the centre of a network of agents who were my senses and perceptions. What was I missing while I was away? My mother wrote repeatedly but she couldn't be expected to tell me the things I wanted to know or even to divine that I might like to know them. I examined every word, even her handwriting, to see if I could detect any difference from her former style, read anything behind the phrases that had slipped in unobserved. There was nothing: only the same even, humorous tone laced with affection for me that she'd always used.

It was getting hotter in Iticino. When I went back I'd have to be more careful. For I mustn't collapse again. I must keep awake to understand, like the times I'd tried not to fall asleep on the farm in order to listen to the conversation below and had felt myself drifting, realized with a jerk that I'd missed something, concentrated and finally lost out. I was older now and there were things I must know. "It's not love, Kit," said Jude and, "We have fallen in love," answered my mother. Yet I couldn't quite make clear in my mind what it was that I was trying to find out. Maybe like all good discussion it would make itself clear:

the means was also end. I knew only that in myself a sub-
terranean debate was going on, of which, like those conversations eavesdropped on the verge of sleep, I heard only
a part and couldn't even be sure what size part.

The proposed dinner at Ellie's had taken place. I was
sorry to have missed that. The discussions too had gone on
without me; my mother sent me resumés with the chief
points attributed. I wrote to Gerry. Above all I was concerned that she shouldn't leave. I must get better quickly.
I must give no cause for alarm to Grand'mère, who was
probably in constant touch with my parents. Restrained
but cheerful, energetic without any suspicion of frenzy:
that was how a child should be. Not too much exercise
had been the doctor's orders but I mustn't seem to be
moping about. It was true that I could breathe more easily
in the rarer atmosphere at Grand'mère's; in Iticino I had
felt my face swathed in a blanket like a cere cloth and the
breath like a tennis ball lodged in my chest. There was
even a danger that the sharper northern air itself might
lead to a telltale overflow of exhilaration.. I must watch my
step very carefully. I felt like a fighter pilot being rested
from combat duty, chafing to get back on ops and knowing
I should have to pass the stiffest medical of all time: the
hawk eyes of my mother's concern.

Grand'mère was pleased to find me alternately reading docilely and jumping up puppy-eager for a walk. She
saw no harm in my reading matter, nor would the strictest
nineteenth-century puritan parent have done. Harm is not
in-dwelling. Like beauty it's in the eye of the beholder. I
have been more deeply influenced towards the offbeat by
John Milton than by John Lennon. Not for hundreds of

years have those lascivious tales been considered anything other than myth and therefore innocuous. To me they were inflammatory, anarchic, and entirely seductive. At last I was to be released from my wooden coffin cradle, for such it seemed to me those pine forests beyond the little city were, and be sent forth like all the messianic children to bring not peace but a sword. It wasn't the plane that flew me south but I who carried the plane forward. The other passengers needn't have worried had they known. My will wouldn't have let them down.

My mother and Ajax met me at the airport with the car and a suitable display of delight. The difference I hadn't been able to extract from her letters I drew at once from their presence, as strong and spiced as her perfume. They had grown together like the red rose and the briar, an unmistakeable entwined intimacy no doubt sprung from sharing the same bed. It was as if at moments their very flesh melted together or was diffused in an ectoplasmic cloud between them so that although their hands didn't touch it seemed that they did or that the table that separated them conveyed a current from one to the other by which they were bound like an invisible umbilical cord. I knew they'd been sleeping together while I'd been away; not just a quick in and out but lying in each other's arms all night, their breath in unison, their limbs and very pulses blending until they became one.

My first job was to see Gerry but it was clear that my comings and goings would be more difficult now.

"Take it easy for a bit," said my father. "Your mother's been very worried about you. We all have."

"I'm fine. Honestly. Didn't Grand'mère tell you?"

"Well, don't undo all your good work and hers," my father answered ambiguously though the ambiguity was mine not his. I decided to take his advice. But I must see Gerry.

"Perhaps not the bar tonight?" my mother said after dinner.

"I'd rather like some fresh air," I said. "It's a bit stuffy after the north, especially indoors. I think I'd sleep better if I felt fresher."

She looked anxious but she gave way. "Alright, just for half an hour." I hid my triumph not only in the small victory but in my own ability to win, my cunning.

Even as we approached the piazza I could see Leo sitting by himself at the back of the pavement and hear the plucked and strummed notes seemingly incoherent and yet not discordant as if they unwound some thread of thought meanderings among the labyrinthine chairs and tables. When we were settled at a table I went over to him and stood so that my back blocked any view of my actions from my own party.

"Hi kid! Long time!" Leo looked up but went on strumming.

"Hi. I been away for a bit; got sick."

"So I heard. You take it all too hard; let them put it over on you. Still it's hard when you're only a kid. You want to hightail out to freedom. That's the way to be healthy."

"Maybe when I'm older."

"You're an alright kid. It's civilisation that's the shit."

"I have to get in touch with Gerry."

"Yeah, she wondered if you'd ever show again."

"I wrote her. Anyway I'm here now. Can you take this to her?" I dug a note from inside my shirt.

"I'm not a messenger boy, kid."

"I know but I can't get up there. They're watching me." I dug in my shirt again. "Look, I haven't got any pot but take this." I pushed a ten dollar bill at him.

"This your old man's?"

"It was. He gave it me. I can have it when I like." Leo folded up the note. "Okay. I take it as a token of how desperate you are and because money don't mean nothing."

"I gotta go back. Will you do it for me?"

"Alright, kid, alright. Stay cool. She'll get it tonight." I had asked Gerry to meet me the next day at the bar. Now I went back to the others and took up my pose, tilting my chair back on two legs and letting my long pale fingers toy with my glass like any nineties dark angel. Soon my mother signalled our exit. At our door Ajax said goodnight and roared off up the hill. When I had gotten into bed there was a tap on the door. It would be my mother, I knew. Tonight was to be mine. Was it because I hadn't seen her for so long that she looked even more beautiful? Or was it something different, an unaccustomed ease? I lay back against the pillows, a sheet drawn over me watching her as she talked, asking me about Grand'mère, telling me of the places they'd visited in my absence, adding to her letters. Suddenly I was very tired. I smiled but she seemed a long way away.

"You're sleepy. Goodnight, darling. It's nice to have you back." When she was gone and the room dark I listened for imagined sounds in the garden but it was very still with the foliage pricked in its turn for murmurs from the house, green fleshy cactus ears, frond antennae, leathery elephant lobes of the fig tree.

The heat woke me early but I stayed in bed hearing the day get under way in the villa and the little town, distant indistinct cries, the clop and rumble that meant a cart, the saw mill of insect life. It always surprised me that there were no tree locusts like those that screamed around the Massachusetts farm but maybe the trees weren't high enough or the olives too tough and bitter. When I judged it a respectable hour I dressed and went down, drank my coffee slowly, and even allowed the signora to persuade me to eat a roll. I was a model of rationality.

"Are you going out, darling?" my mother asked.

"Down to the piazza. I have to meet a friend." I wanted to begin to establish Gerry in their minds. "We're not recording today, are we?"

"What shall we call ourselves?" my father laughed.

"The Little Fishes," I suggested.

"Who knows, perhaps we shall make the number-one spot."

"And what'll we call the record?"

"The end of the world?" I said and then could have bitten my tongue out at my mother's anxious look. "Or Yes, we have no future today," I went on with a kind of recklessness now that the first slip had been made.

"Who's your friend?" asked Ajax with an attempt at diversion we were all grateful for but particularly me.

"Gerry. She's from the States. She's moved into the Albergo. Got tired of bumming it." I looked at my wristwatch. "I'd better go or I'll miss her." I was all smiles and eagerness again. I felt their tension relax, waved and ran out into the already molten sunshine that filled the narrow streets like lava. I was early but the chance to get out was too good.

However I'd hardly had a moment to properly assume the young Rimbaud before Gerry appeared. Rimbaud is a good character to take for sitting alone. He allows one to be perfectly possessed without demanding the heightened idiosyncrasy of a Wilde or a Firbank which is best kept for after dark. She came almost running down the cobbled street; the Indian sandals bravely flashed and her breasts bobbed becomingly so that the loungers shouted their appreciation at each other as if she were deaf or a specially fine squid displayed on a stall. I was glad her Italian was so poor. Even through the blurring of dialect she might have understood and I didn't want her driven away just yet.

She was quite breathless and the sweat stood in little molehills on her forehead. "Jesus, I thought you were never coming back."

"I wrote you."

"I know but you're just a kid you might have changed your mind or just not been able to."

"I am so weary of being told I'm only a child. It really is in no way my fault that I was born so little time ago."

"I'm sorry, Kit. Don't get sore."

I waved at the waiter. "What do you want to drink or don't you accept drinks from a child."

"I'll have a pressed lemon."

I'd reduced her to dependence.

"Jon's gone and Okie," she said looking a little forlornly across the square. "I ought to pull myself together and go too. I'm such a mess."

"You look better," I offered.

"Oh on the outside I'm clean but inside . . ."

"What happened to Jon?"

"He went up to Paris. There's someone up there, an old musician, who gives him money. Maybe he'll come back."

"And Okie?"

"He met up with another like him who was going to make his way to Sweden where they've got some big thing going for U.S. deserters." As ever the poverty of Gerry's expression hit me making me miss some of the content. "Did you know Leo's a war veteran?" I shook my head. "Korean war. He was wounded, too. He gets some kind of a pension. I reckon he's nearly forty but you can't tell with that emaciated face he has and the straggly hair all over. I admire Leo. I really do."

"He's all mixed up."

"Yeah but sometimes he's almost saintly with it. It's a way of life."

"It always has been since the desert fathers."

"Oh and the Jewish sects."

"And Diogenes," I said. "How far back do you want to go?"

"I admire it so much. It's in India too," she said looking down at her sandals. "But I can't do it. I don't know what'll become of me. I have to find some compromise or I can't live with myself. I can't just go back and pretend there's nothing else. You're so lucky."

"How come?"

"You're international. You don't have to come to terms with your culture."

"Well, you don't have to go home yet. There's plenty of time."

"I guess you're pretty mixed up too. You must be to be hooked so young. I know how you feel. I have this desire to be at peace, to be done with it all; for nothing. Nirvana—isn't that the most beautiful word?"

"It means a blowing out," I said.

"Like a candle. That's beautiful too. How do you know?"

"My mother told me. Sanskrit's one of her things."

Gerry sighed again. "You see, I'll never know enough. How could I ever raise children when I know so little."

I passed her an envelope across the table. "In there's some rent to be going on with. I think it makes us up to date. I'll let you have more as and when."

She put out a hand. "Gee I hate to take money from you."

"As Leo says: money's nothing."

"Our whole society's based on it," she said morosely. "And yet that isn't what most of us want and it doesn't make us happy."

"Happy?"

"Don't you believe it's possible to be happy?"

"I don't know if I know what it means or what you mean by it."

"Maybe all we want, any of us, is love."

"What's that?"

"I guess you're too young. Maybe I am too. But at least I believe it exists."

"Do you love Jon?"

"I don't know. Yes, a little. That is, I'm very fond of him."

"That's all there is; that and sex."

"No, there's something else. I know."

"That's like believing in God."

"I know that's how it seems but it's different somehow." A shadow fell across our table. We had both been looking down into our glasses to avoid each other's eyes.

"*Ciao*, Kit! *Come stai?*" It was Gennaro.

"*Ciao!* Gerry, Gennaro." They shook hands. I knew he had come across for that. "I have to go," I said to Gerry. "*Devo andare.*" I added to Gennaro, "See you." I got up and walked away wondering how they would get on without a common language. I heard the scrape of my chair as he sat down in it. At the other edge of the piazza I looked back and waved. They waved back and then their eyes encountered and they began the dance of the damsel flies. For that is all it is: two evanescents on a hot afternoon; meaningless and not even particularly beautiful—a commonplace of nature.

I felt fine as I walked back. I'd reacclimatized to Iticino very quickly, to its higher pressure and torrid weather. After lunch we all drove in to Naples, my father at the wheel with Ajax beside him while I sat in the back inhaling my mother's perfumed warmth. We fought our way up and down Via Roma for the luxuries of civilised living Iticino couldn't provide. Ajax hadn't really seen Naples on our way down so my father played *cicerone*.

"The old Bourbon station used to be quite handsome but they pulled it down to have a modern one like Rome and Milan," my mother said. It was one of the rare moments when she spoke to Ajax and always it was to give harmless textbook information. Did she know I was watching or was that all there was to it? Perhaps by now their dance was over and I'd missed it through my weakness. As ever the people in the streets turned to stare and chatter after us. One man was so astounded he nearly walked into an oncoming tram but the irate clanging woke him in time.

"Italy has become so bourgeois," my father said. "That's what happens when you improve the material standards of an agricultural peasantry. It's hard to see it as the land of the Renaissance and the Baroque. Everyone wants to be respectable. It's a very real danger."

"That's why you have people like Leo," I said. We had found a good restaurant and were having dinner before going back.

"Who's Leo, darling?"

"The hippy who plays the guitar."

"Youthful protest." My father nipped the end off a breadstick with his strong white teeth.

"Oh he's not young. He was in the Korean war. He must be nearly thirty-five or even more."

"One of the original Beats," said Ajax.

We drove back in the dark, the headlights picking out the cliff face, then spearing into tempting velvety abyss as Ajax steered the car down the last stretches of coast road. Out, as I judged, at sea small lights gleamed, perhaps Gennaro casting a net. My mother sat beside Ajax.

"Does it worry you driving in the dark," I asked from behind.

"No, not really."

"It's very beautiful," said my mother.

> " 'If it were now to die
> 'Twere now to be most happy, for, I fear,
> My soul hath her content so absolute,
> That not another comfort like to this
> Succeeds in unknown fate . . .' "

The words were spoken very quietly but firmly as my mother's lover peered ahead down the twin track of the headlights; so quietly that I wondered if I'd invented them or rather the saying of them.

Next morning Ajax had already arrived when I came down. As I carried my coffee through from the kitchen I heard the two low voices, my mother's and her lover's, as I pushed the living room door open. They were standing very close together and my eye registered the blurred end of a movement that might have meant they had been holding hands.

"Hello, darling." She turned to me. "What are you going to do this morning?"

"I thought I might have a swim."

"Would you mind if I came too," Ajax asked. Had I almost caught a look between them?

"That'd be fine."

"I'll go up and change then. I should be back by the time you finish your coffee."

"Where's Paw?" I asked when Ajax had gone.

"Giving Renata an English lesson on the *terrazza*," my mother answered. "You'll see them when you take your cup back," she smiled.

I grinned. She has the ability to read my thoughts more than anyone else. Often she knows which side of the line, child/adult, I'm going to play it. When she does of course I usually play child to disarm her but I'm not sure if it works always. This time I took the cup through. Even without looking out I could now hear voices from the terrace. Why had I missed them before? I'd been too busy in my own mind, that was it, and it was dangerous. That way you could miss a lot. I heard the car come back with Ajax.

We left our clothes in two heaps side by side on the beach and waded out. The water was warm and sticky as a thermal bath and the angled sun poured down on the glassy surface that became a huge polished reflector bouncing back dazzle and heat as if from a continuous fission.

"I'm going to swim round the point. What about you?" Ajax threw water over bare shoulders to damp down the sun flare. As we pushed through the shallows still only thigh deep I felt that the water slipped past my thin body whereas Ajax' stocky truculence thrust it away. "I'll take my time. I'm not in training like you are."

At once I dived. Ajax was there to keep an eye on me. I meant to make it hard. Should I give a warning about the currents at the tip? I decided not and drew away from the stolid figure calmly breasting the water. As I felt the pull near the point I set myself to beat it without seeming to. Once I looked back. Ajax was only a little behind and seemed in no hurry. Then I was out of sight. I put everything I could into a spurt. When I looked round again Ajax' head was bobbing seal-like, black against the alabaster sky and aquamarine water. Perhaps my own effort had drained the colour from them. I made a last push as if I were trying to escape, staggered up and flung myself face down on the sand, my skin prickling on the burning grains so that I lay on a bed of desired pain resistless, waiting for what should come out of the sea. I kept my face turned down so that I couldn't see an imagined Ajax striding out of the water and falling on me. I would be too exhausted to fight back.

"That's quite a current round the end." A heavy drop of water fell on my dried hot skin. I moved my head a little and opened an eye. Ajax was standing beside me. I could reach out and touch. More warm splashes fell on me from Ajax' shaken hair. I could see the ribcage heaving with labored breaths. But Ajax was strong and stood there in the sunlight sewn over with droplets that flashed like fish scales. All strength went out of me, a tide flowing through my hollow body to leave me stranded and empty. Ajax sat down on the beach. After a moment I turned over, warding the light from my eyes with a hand.

Before I'd been too taken up to look around for Leo.

"Who lives there?" asked Ajax.

"That's Honeymoon Hotel," I said, "for those who want to take their clothes off for each other. That's the fire."

Ajax got up and went to examine the blackened spot. "It's no warmer than anywhere else on this beach. Do we have to swim back?"

"No, we can go over the top." I nodded towards the spit of rocks.

"I think it'd better be soon. I shall fry out here."

"There's nobody about anyway. I'd have introduced you. Leo's alright but he's a bit abrasive."

"He might be in the Hotel."

"If he is he's sleeping off a trip and it's not good to wake him. But he might have hitched into Naples to stock up."

Ajax nodded. "Well, if you're rested I'd like to get back to my shirt. I don't much want to be flayed alive tonight. You lead the way but have respect for my great age. I'm out of training for mountaineering."

"Why do you think they do it?" I asked as we walked towards the rocks.

"Opt out?"

"Yes."

"It seems to be a constant thread in human history, so that suggests a psychological rather than a social or historical reason. There are always plenty of reasons lying around in organized society for getting out of it. Some do, some don't. I suspect it may be a kind of masochism though it'd take some time to work that out in detail."

We scrambled over the rocks, my mother's lover wincing as uncalloused feet and hands met the rough surfaces. I smiled secretly in the lead, pleased with my own toughness. As we climbed down the other side I saw that two large and two small figures had joined our clothes. Even from a distance with the unfocusing glare of the water I recognized Ellie and the children with Caspar Melchitz, one of her most patient conductors, his dark Arab features setting off her full blondness as if someone had co-starred Valentino and Monroe. It was rumoured that was why she so often appeared with him. We dropped down into the water and splashed towards them.

"Hi, you're quite the outdoor type," Ellie greeted Ajax.

"Only with Kit," said my mother's lover.

"We wondered whose the clothes were."

Ajax slipped into the cotton shirt with relief.

"Is that modesty? It can't be that you're cold."

I grinned inside. I'd seen Ellie's performance so often.

"The opposite."

"Ajax is very afraid of getting burned," I said. "How are you, Caspar?"

"How are you? When I asked for you at dinner your mother said you were sick."

"I'm fine. Too much sun that was all. I'm a worshipper," I said.

"We must go," said Ellie. "Come on, kids."

"I'm hungry," said Karen.

"Me too," the boy echoed.

"See you!"

"*Ciao!*"

"You were rather short with her," I said when they'd gone and we were dressed.

"Was I?"

"What did you think of Caspar?"

"We met at dinner. I liked him. I've never heard him conduct. Is he good?"

"Not bad. He's good with Ellie; takes a very firm line with her. That's mainly why she sticks with him. He won't let her throw a temperament. Makes her rehearse. Then she gets good notices, they're snapped dancing together and an Italian magazine says what a handsome couple and that's all good for publicity. It's happened so often you'd think the newspapers would be on to it by now."

"So he isn't her boyfriend. I thought . . ."

I broke in with a laugh. "Caspar knows her too well. It's useful to them both. But he likes more mind. He's always had a big thing for mother. You probably noticed." I flicked my towel at Ajax' shadow on the sand without looking up. My mother's lover didn't answer.

"We saw Ellie," I said later at lunch. "And Caspar looking his usual devilishly handsome self."

My mother and father both laughed. "That was very well turned, darling," she said. Again I didn't look at Ajax.

Yet it's only now that I remember I didn't look; it's hindsight again. And indeed I'm not sure I even knew at that point how much was behind my actions. There's a space between unconscious and conscious, a space of becoming, where you do and say, as it used to be called, and still is by some school teachers, I believe, thoughtlessly or even better heedlessly, and if questioned in a court of law, "Did you know what you were doing?" you could answer with equal truth either yes or no.

Renata came along with us to the bar that evening. Her mother had been suddenly called after dinner and had risen up leaving all like a Christian with a vision. Ajax led the way with Renata's heels clapping alongside like the hooves of one of the small local donkeys; we followed in an unholy trinity. I couldn't see my mother's face in the dark. Leo was there with the newest batch of wandering boys and girls; Gerry too, playing the role of resident matron. I waved and grinned but didn't go over. From across the tables she seemed confident and expansive. Leo was wearing his most impressive swami.

"We have now the vacation," Renata was saying as we sat down. My father didn't seem to have improved her English greatly. "Please," she said, turning to him, "what is the difference between vacation and holidays?"

"Vacation is American; holidays are English."

"What is the meaning of holi?"

"Holy, *santi; giorni festivi.*"

"It is better to say vacation or holidays?"

"It depends which country you're in."

"*Si ma* . . ."

"Yes but . . ." my father corrected.

"Yes but," she said dutifully, "English is more genteel; American is more modern, isn't it?"

"It's not as simple as that."

"To us it seems so."

"You should talk more with Ajax," said my father. "Ajax' English isn't contaminated."

"Contaminated?"

"*Contaminato*, and Ajax doesn't speak Italian." Ajax laughed. I took a quick look at my mother but she seemed engrossed in something across the square and was smoking with her gaze fixed away from us. In a minute she turned towards us.

"Which of those is your friend, darling?"

"That's Gerry: the clean one sitting down. The others are new, apart from Father Leo."

"Father?" questioned Renata.

"It's a joke," said my father.

"I see," she smiled. For a moment there was silence;

Renata sipped her scotch on the rocks. Then she swirled the ice cubes. My father summoned the waiter for another round.

"My turn," said Ajax.

"Why are they boums?" asked Renata when fresh drinks had come, looking distastefully at Leo's group who were now listening with rapt faces while he sang "Put your best foot forward man blues," a composition of his own I recognised as the wandering tune he most often picked out when he was alone. "They don't exist in Italy."

"Kit should tell us," said my father.

"They don't like their society and they want freedom." I felt myself hampered by the need to explain myself simply.

Renata pulled a face. "No one is free."

"Americans are brought up on the concept of freedom. It's written into their history and their constitution. It may be all an illusion."

"It's a byproduct of the idea of an economic free-for-all and the puritan conscience," my mother put in.

"It is like a child to try to escape."

"What is important then?" I asked.

"*I soldi.*"

"Money," I explained to Ajax.

"Danae," said my mother.

"There is a painting by Tiziano at Capodimente of Danae and the gold," my father said carefully.

"I have seen with the school. It is very beautiful." I wondered what the signora's reaction would have been, whether she would have accepted the received opinion of the beauty of a nude prostitute.

"I've seen reproductions," said Ajax. "Is it very beautiful?"

"Not to me. But it's very interesting."

"Cupid is turning away," said my father.

"Prostitution drives out love," said my mother.

"Love is for the movies," Renata said.

"Isn't there an old woman?" Ajax asked.

"A sort of nurse-cum-brothelkeeper? That's in the other version; the one that's most often reproduced. She's catching the shower as it falls." My mother shuddered a little.

"What do you think is most important in the life?" Renata looked at my father.

"Power."

"Powere?"

"It's what everyone wants, individually and collectively as nations. Power over ourselves so that we can have power over others. Power and possession."

"Is that what you want, Allthing?" I called him that sometimes to annoy and compliment him together.

"I have them." He picked up his glass in the traditional gesture of immovable self-assurance.

"And you?" my mother asked Ajax.

"I have what I want, only like all greedy children I want more."

With half an eye (which half?) I saw Gennaro on the edge of the square nod to Gerry and her bow her head in an almost bashful acknowledgement. The towel would be out tonight. I would let my mother and her lover be alone and unobserved if they wanted but tomorrow I must see if my route was still working. Like a good general I must inspect. Then it seemed they didn't want my offer. Once again Ajax roared off early and alone. Maybe I'd been right and the dance was over.

In the morning I left them to their discussion and went down to the old shore where Gennaro and I had met as children. I sat on a rock and wondered if Ellie's children or indeed any others would come there, whether the nature of childhood would change. I wrote a sci-fi story in my head for the receptionist at the Albergo del Golfo to read called *The Very Last Child* and designed the jacket with a picture of me on my rock. I supposed that was what Joseph had been doing when he had his dream about everyone bowing down to him, and Robinson Crusoe self-sufficient on his island. Everyone was so old and the world was so old and yet they seemed to me just children and to have hardly begun; their concerns the building of fantasies or follies with toy bricks, their squabbles Tweedledum and dee fights, their desires a fairy story for a wet fireglow evening. I wanted something quite new that no one had ever dirtied with his mind before and for a time I felt that beating in the chest and catch in the throat that meant I was just about to realize it. The rocks stood out like before a storm, slate-blue rimmed as if an electric current hedged them round, against a background of pebbles each one as precise as the pattern in a rug or in the description of a *nouvelle vague* novelist. At any moment! But it didn't come. It never does. I knew that old deception of the senses. I must be careful not to get sunstroke on the shimmering beach.

All that came just as I was about to go away was Gennaro. I hoped I'd drawn him with my mesmeric powers.

He was wearing a shirt open to the navel and light pants; rubber sandals on his bare feet. He exuded confidence and a certain smugness.

"Well?"

"It is good to have a foreign woman. She is very good."

"Don't forget I introduced you."

"You will always be my friend. That other one was a witch."

"I want to go fishing with you." He looked doubtful. "Just the two of us. One night."

"It's difficult."

"Remember the pzzt-pzzt." I squirted an imaginary aerosol at him. "And the American."

"Now she stays at the Albergo it is better."

"All Italians are snobs."

"A man has a reputation."

"*Guaglione*," I sneered. "Take me fishing or I shall tell her you've had many tourist girls."

"Alright, alright."

"Good." I got up. "I'll tell you when."

"Perhaps it isn't a good time for the fish when you say."

"It doesn't matter. We will find something."

"You're mad."

"Yes, I'm mad. See you."

That afternoon I played tired, leaving them all still sitting at table. Soon I heard the car, crept down the stairs, out through the hall and out into the lane. My marks were there at every crossing though I didn't need them, burned into the withered grass like mason's signs carved in stone. I

couldn't see how anyone could fail to spot and follow
them. The honeysuckle was still in blossom; its perfume
muffled by heat and dust. There was no towel. Our car was
out in front.

This time the receptionist wasn't there. On the desk
lay *In Transito Per Venere* with the jacket showing a
beautiful woman modelled on the early vamps. Riskily I
slipped round, lifted the key from its peg, and made for
the stairs. After lunch was a good sleepy time. The receptionist would be chatting or dozing. My heart began its
familiar percussion. There was no cry after me. Suppose
Gerry came back? I had to chance it. I let myself in.

If I hung out the towel Gerry would know I was up
there. But I might be seen on the balcony if Ajax' shutters weren't closed. I sweated with the problem while I lit
my cloudy disguise, this time like a joss stick so I wouldn't
have to draw any in. I blew on the end to keep it going
until the air was spiced, then left it to smoulder out on the
ashtray. In a little while I had shut myself in the bathroom, taken off my shoes, and mounted the john; poised
like Cupid on a plinth though with a pocket knife instead
of bow and arrow in my mischievous grasp.

It was clear as soon as the periscope was in position
that I'd missed most of the A feature. My mother and
Ajax lay together hardly stirring except for a small gesture
from a hand or a whispered word. Sometimes Ajax would
lightly kiss my mother's breast or temples and she would
respond with a movement or a smile. Their mutual tenderness and absorption was almost frightening. I was angry
with myself for being so slow. I wanted to shake the kaleidoscope and change the picture. I wanted action, not this

dreaming calm. My mother was as beautiful as ever. Ajax looked very young and vulnerable lying in a childish nakedness. I replaced the covers and got down. There was nothing else to do. I might as well get out before they began to stir or Gerry came back.

She was in fact coming through the door as I hit the bottom of the stairs. I called, "Hi!" quickly and beckoned her over. I manoeuvered her to stand with her back to the desk and gave her the key. We said goodbye loudly and then I went quickly out into the safety of the lane. As I passed the car I was tempted to let a tyre down or put it in gear.

By the honeysuckle I paused and looked up. Gerry seemed to be hanging out swimming things. The next-door shutters were still closed. What would they do? Perhaps they'd sleep, their sweat running together. It was very hot and very quiet in the lane. Even the cicadas wilted in silence among the crackling stalks. Maybe they felt their paper wings and husk bodies might take instant fire if they moved. I laughed at the thought of a grasshopper striking a spark from his rubbed twig legs and setting the whole coast alight. Now I'd have to take another risk—that there was no one in the garden. It was safer than going in through the front door. I thrust against the back door in the wall. It gave with a small crack. I was inside and had pushed it to behind me almost without thinking. With my back flat against it, the hot wood burning through my shirt like St. Lawrence's grate, I studied the terrain. I picked up a stick at my feet, nicked it and put it behind my back where I fingered it through the hoops so that I needn't take my gaze from the apparently empty garden and the window eyes of the house. Anyone watching would have found it hard to follow the sequence of actions and understand what I was doing. I walked calmly towards the kitchen. A cicada plopped heavily out of my path. Nothing else moved.

All the rest of the day I was very cheerful so that when I said I was going to bed early no one should think I was sulking. I knew it wouldn't be long before there was a tap on the door.

"Hello, darling, just came to see if you were alright."

"I'm fine, thanks."

She sat down on the bed. "What're you reading?"

"Thought I'd better do a bit of work at my Latin. It's getting very rusty and I don't know when I might need it." I pushed the book towards her. "I thought I might do a verse translation but I don't know."

"Ovid? He's a prosy old thing."

"He's full of stories though."

"Oh yes, he's a marvellous source book. Where are you up to?"

"Book ten. Venus and Adonis." For a moment I thought some shade crossed her face. "Isn't it really the same story as Diana and Actaeon?"

"How do you mean, darling?"

"Well, if Ajax is right and they're all the one goddess only in slightly different aspects then it's all the same lover too. And it even says here that Venus went hunting like Diana, and the deaths are much the same. There's one thing, though."

"What's that?" She moved a strand of hair from my

eyes. "You ought to cut some of that. Soon you won't be able to see out."

I tossed my head. "The hounds that kill Actaeon and lure Adonis away."

" 'Lure him away?' "

"Look, it says it was the hounds that led him to the boar." I put my finger on the lines.

"Yes."

"What are they?"

"Their own desires."

"Is there something about the goddess then that causes the death of her lovers."

"I hope not."

"What is it then?"

She thought a moment. "Actaeon wanted her when she didn't want him so his own desires made him a hunted thing and destroyed him."

"And Adonis?"

"That's more difficult. He seems to have defied love and desired death. Both of them sinned against the goddess or perhaps they wanted her in her more deathly form as Persephone." My mother was no longer talking to me but to herself. "If so the fault was theirs, not hers. There is one version where it's Diana who sends the boar which would make Adonis exactly parallel with Actaeon, perhaps wanting more than he could have."

"In the *Metamorphoses* she was on her way to Cyprus, so maybe he was just killing time hunting."

My mother winced. "That was a nasty image, darling."

"Maybe the moral is that goddesses shouldn't fall in love or you with them."

"Perhaps. What about a little sleep?"

"Okay." I smiled my sleepy ingenuous child smile and snuggled down under the sheet, a good action for making one seem helpless, recalling as it does the cot and the hospital bed.

"Shall I put the light out?"

"Not just now. I want to think a bit."

"You won't be too long, will you? It'll be late tomorrow with Ellie and Caspar coming to dinner. They always stay hours. That was a very good joke of yours today."

"About his devilish handsomeness?"

"Yes."

"Like an Arab."

"That's right, Valentino." She laughed. "Goodnight, darling."

"Night."

When she'd gone I read again in Ovid: "*caelo praefertur Adonis.*" She prefers Adonis to heaven. I'd been wrong. The dance wasn't over. They had kidded themselves they were in love. But it didn't exist, that state. It was for myth and fairy tale, to give people something to dream about and to explain things for psychiatrists.

They were on time for once, at least once for Ellie, who always arrived late and breathless. I wondered how she ever came in on time but maybe Caspar took charge of both kinds of entrance. He came directly up to my mother, kissed her, and took her hand. "It's lovely to see you. You look marvellous as usual. Other women come to the south to tan their skins to hide; you remain Victorianly white as if you were always under the parasol."

"I'm a nocturnal animal," my mother laughed. "I can just about tolerate moonlight."

"Then I must show you to the moon."

"And I should complain about the cold. What will you have to drink?" She moved him towards the table where Ajax was pouring aperitifs. My father refuses to adopt the American custom of cocktails, calling them both dangerous and phony, a term which he uses only in extreme cases and as if he had just discovered or invented it. We serve drinks almost crude; even ice has to be asked after.

"A lot of soda, a whole ocean," Ellie was crying. "Alcohol is so bad for my voice, isn't it, Caspar? Why, that's lovely. Just the right touch. My you have marvellous hands. Hasn't Ajax got marvellous hands." And Ellie took the hand of my mother's lover. "Now if I were a fortune teller I'd know everything about you." With one finger she began to trace the lines on the palm holding it so that it couldn't escape. Ajax stood smiling but a little stiff. "Don't you think I have some gypsy in me? My maternal grandmother was Hungarian. Don't you feel the beating of my wild Magyar blood?" She was in full flight now in her Southern belle role, a cross between Tosca and Scarlett O'Hara. Ajax' hand was withdrawn so gently she hardly noticed it go.

"I can't say you look very gypsy," said my father.

"Oh you're so literal always. I can be anything I want. Can't I be anything I want?" she appealed this time as Shirley Temple in *The Bluebird*. You will wonder how I'm able to recognise these performances. When Fantah and I are alone on the farm we watch the late movie while the insects beat themselves to death against the wire meshed porch. Fantah finds the mythology of old movies more exotic than the young Krishna among the cow girls. I've often thought the local farmers mistake her for an escaped Red Indian when she's shopping in the drive-in supermarket. She is also deeply moved by Howard Johnson's Disney dwarf plastic ice cream parlours as we drive about the countryside and cries and claps her hands at their orange roofs as at the most beautiful Jain temples. I don't think she's ever dared go inside one. She says it is all part of native culture and must be studied to understand the society. It may be that Ellie is older than she lets on, more than the couple of years she lets her friends know she takes off for the journalists, that she too knows so many old roles or maybe there's an Ellie who lies alone at night on a silk chaise longue nibbling a narcissistic little something and watching the blurred old prototypes caper in front of her. Why do I hate Ellie? Is it because she treats me as a child except when she wants to use me? When they are older I may, with a little turn of the screw, subvert her children.

The signora had a village child to help her serve, a girl of the age Renata had been when we first knew her. I wondered how Renata was passing her evening. Ellie sat on my father's right; Caspar on my mother's. Ajax was opposite Ellie; I was on my mother's left: a table arrangement I couldn't have bettered given the players. What would we play; psychological strip poker? Caspar led with the soup.

"And what have you been doing with yourself, Kit?"

"Brushing up my Latin."

"Kit's been reading the *Metamorphoses*."

"Which part?"

"Venus and Adonis."

"There's a story I'd like someone to make an opera of."

"And I could sing Venus," Ellie put in from her end. "Otto could play Cupid in a wisp of something."

"As long as he didn't have to sing," said Caspar. "It's remarkable how both your children seem to be tone deaf."

"I don't know what they'll do when they're older. It's terrible to be a mother."

"There's plenty of time," said Ajax, "before you need worry."

"I don't know. We've gotten so career conscious that if you're not down for something before you're through grade school you're beginning to think you're a social misfit." There are times when Ellie likes to play the suburban mother as though she hadn't international stardom and a matching bank balance. "What're you going to do, Kit?"

"Nothing rather elegantly." Ellie looked shocked. "Why does one always have to do something?"

"To live," said Caspar.

"Isn't it more important to be?"

"If you're as pretty as a butterfly," he said. I've long thought that Caspar doesn't really like me. His opening question had been not because he cared but to be thought to be showing an interest.

My mother jumped to my defence. "Surely Kit's right. Isn't it a legacy of puritanism that makes us so guilt-ridden about work?"

"We'll all have to learn to do a great deal less of it in time," said my father. I could hear the work statistics data beginning to punchcard through his head. At any minute he would be spewing them out all over the table like ticker tape.

"Maybe I'll run an international review or go around the world organizing protests."

Caspar shook his head. "It's not so easy."

"We've become so much more insular. Every country is an island," said my father. "Russia and America with their satellites are archipelagos and the rest are islands. All the little bits of Africa and Asia, all islets and atolls, all breaking up and gathering their little bit of sea, their ethnic and cultural differences round them."

"Hasn't it always been so?" Caspar asked, crumbling his bread.

"I don't think so, I don't think so." My father was becoming excited and pronounced all his consonants almost as z's. "I think there was more cultural homogeneity in the Middle Ages, the Renaissance, the early part of this century. When suddenly we have become one species in face of space travel, in science, in everything else we have reverted to tribal bands. Are we afraid to lose our pitiful individuality or are we played upon by politicians? Look at France. She has become a deep pocket of nothing. She makes me weep."

"And Italy?" said Caspar.

"It is better not to say," said my father as the signora entered with a steaming dish of hunter's chicken. "We are all provincial these days."

"Even America?"

"Especially America. She is a monstrous child of the mid-nineteenth century when men were first hit by technology and imperialism." My father was very emphatic.

"Blintz and the devil had done for the rest," I quoted Fantah. Caspar frowned.

"Is the replacement of French by English as the international language only a symptom or something more radical?" asked Ajax.

"It's an effect that in its turn becomes a cause, isn't it?" my mother said.

"My, it's all so difficult," Ellie sighed.

"Don't worry. Music remains international," Caspar consoled her. "We're unlikely to be out of a job."

"Work again," I said. "You're all so traditional."

"Do your friends on the beach have a better answer?" asked my father.

"Oh them. They're as traditional as you only they're anti matter."

"What then?"

"You'll see."

My mother laughed. "Yes, we will."

"And Venus and Adonis?" asked my mother's lover.

"Adonis is always destroyed."

"But he rises again, doesn't he?" Caspar was determined to keep me in my place this evening. "He's a fertility god, isn't he?"

"Adoni, my Lord," my mother looked deep into her glass. We were drinking a heavy red local wine that the signora prescribed for her patients after childbirth. "*Fa sangue,*" she always said in incantation. "It was originally an eastern cult."

"Oh but northern as well; Tacitus described it," put in my father quickly, always anxious that the North shouldn't be thought to lack its share of any important manifestation.

"Is that so?" Caspar seemed a little incredulous.

"Yes, yes. The goddess went about the country visiting attended by a priest who was probably thought of as her lover. She brought fertility. It's obviously the same. They sacrificed people to her by hanging. I've often thought that's why northern countries kept that form of punishment so long."

"It's a very crude version," said Ellie.

"That's because it's the original rite unembellished by a mythical or artistic dress."

"You're always digging about in these things." Ellie was a little petulant. "Where does it get you?"

"It helps me understand humanity," said my father heavily. "Partly it is my job and partly I think it necessary if we are not to rush like lemmings into some sea of destruction."

"You're always so gloomy, too, like Hamlet. The gloomy Dane," Ellie teased. "And what do you think?" she turned to Ajax, who had been following the conversation with a smiling interest.

"I think everything the human race has ever said or thought or done is a vast communal unconscious we have to bring to the surface and analyse to understand ourselves now. So you see I'm just as bad," Ajax grinned in an attempt to mollify.

"Sometimes," my mother had a wicked gleam in her

eye, "Venus was bearded. It'll be hard to sing wearing a false beard."

"There, Ellie, what about that?" Caspar was delighted.

"Oh you're all too awful. One minute you're so serious, the next . . . I just can't keep up with you."

"A bearded woman and a beardless boy," my mother went on.

"Oh stop it now. You'll put me right off."

"I haven't known you to be so scornful of a beardless boy," said Caspar. "Remember Graz or was it Tel Aviv?"

"Tel Aviv," Ellie reminisced. "And there isn't a whisker on my face. Feel." She tilted her chin at Ajax.

"I'll take your word for it."

"Speaking of faces," I grinned at Caspar, "Mother said you looked like Valentino."

"Looked?"

"Look," I corrected. I knew my mother wouldn't come back with my original comment.

"Does that indicate a wish to be carried off to my tent in the desert?"

"In your character as one of the Four Horsemen of the Apocalypse?" she asked. Caspar lowered his head, acknowledging defeat. Some of Ajax' wine had spilt on the tablecloth, opening in the red ragged petals of dropping anemones as it seeped through the white fabric.

"Why such androgynous figures?" Ellie asked.

"So that they can be all things to all men," said my father.

"So that we can see behind the surface and say: 'You,

you, I want you,' " my mother answered, "without the limitation of the appearance of things."

"In your version, Allthing, Adonis' resurrection is in a new body to be sacrificed in its turn."

"Many lovers but only one goddess," he passed the carafe of wine round the table. Wherever it was set down it left a circular red wound.

"So the madonna had to be all things to all men," Ajax poured more blood into the half empty glass. "Queen of Heaven, peasant girl, mother, and maiden. And now?"

"Now we each have to make our own private mythology," said my mother.

And that's what I'm doing of course. Now that the saints and angels have withdrawn into the "Heaven that never was" and Olympus' slopes are clothed with Euro-tours and Diana raped by a lunar module we must make our pantheon where we can. Mostly we make heroes of bandits and freedom fighters, the lawless who enjoy a god-like freedom and immunity until their glorious deaths—Robin Hood Kelly and Che Hercules. But these are popular legends. I will have a shrine of my own where I am tender priest and worshipper and this is my Bible, the shimmering myth of my own invention.

Ever since we had first come to Iticino I had wanted to go fishing. I had known it wouldn't be allowed so I'd never mentioned it. Now I'd decided I was old enough to make it happen; perhaps I was too old for it to be important. Well, then, I would drown my childhood and catch a monster, a coelocanth, half man-half fish, my own self's Caliban. "Tonight," I told Gennaro.

"You are crazy. There will be no fish."

"It doesn't matter. I will pay for the juice."

"Tonight I have things to do."

"Prss, prss!" I squirted at him. He leaped like one of Pavlov's dogs.

"Alright, alright."

"Once only and then it's done," I calmed.

"Let's hope so."

"Bring some nets."

"Hah!"

Dinner I begged off with the excuse that I was meeting Gerry. "*Ciao!*" I called, putting my head round the door. Later I might say, when I was safely back, where I'd really been. They might meet her when they went out and then I'd have to tell. By then it wouldn't matter except that they would see my mask slither a little like a pure snow slope settling treacherously; not yet an avalanche, just a slide that would hardly perceptibly alter the contours of the landscape but still enough to make them consider. As I went out I felt my mother's concern bat after me like a great moth but I shrugged it off.

"My father would kill me if he knew." Gennaro was waiting beside the long quay.

"No, you're his eldest son. Come on, let's go." There was no one about.

"If anyone saw me . . ."

"Calm down. What did you tell Gerry?"

"Feesh."

"Your English is improving. Did you bring some nets?"

"A small one. We mustn't be seen." He was almost paranoid in his shame. An occasional lamp gleamed along the wall. "Down." He pointed to some steps and led the way to the water. At the bottom a boat knocked very gently against the concrete. It was a little bigger than a rowing boat with an outboard motor over the stern and two big goggle-eyed lamps on either side of the bow. The wood was kippered by long use and I stepped among the coarse weed of net. Gennaro cast off and jerked the motor into life. I shoved against the quay as we drove for the dark. Out there air and water were warm black molasses. The quay was left, a long floating light spar blobbed with the lamps. Above, a few white fallen stars marked the village climbing the hill. As we drew away both we and the village shrank while the seasky gaped like the hot black whale belly for Jonah or Pinocchio.

"How do you steer?"

Gennaro pointed up towards the pied smudge of the Albergo not bothering to speak through the sputter of the motor. I felt a delightful fear suck at me in the enormity of the night. We were dwindling so quickly it must be only a moment before we went out, snuffed between the sooty finger and thumb. If the little engine broke down there were oars but I felt we might row forever and make no progress, held back by an invisible chain on whose end as anchor rode a grinning seahag.

I'd been afraid that, at last achieved, the experience would fail me. Now I realised that in place of the forbiddenness that I'd quivered to before was this frisson of fright, sharp enough to be real yet not overwhelming. I wasn't disappointed. It could be stimulated and controlled in a delicious escalation, a coitus interruptus of fear, sweet brinkmanship. We wedged our way further into the black-furred Sargasso until I could no longer see the beacon of the Albergo when Gennaro cut the engine. The hot, thick silence was almost stifling.

"Can you still see the light?"

"Yes. I have cat's eyes."

"What do we do now?"

"We wait a little for the noise to go away. Then we switch on the lights. But there are no fish."

"Why?"

"It is too early, too hot, the current is wrong."

"It doesn't matter. Switch on the lights." The night seemed to me to have soaked up every sound for miles like inky blotting paper. I wondered why there were no stars. There must be a pall of heat haze.

"You don't switch on," said Gennaro scornfully. The lamps were kerosene burning. The rowboat had become a gondola or itself a fish with luminous eyes in whose gaze insects began to twist and flitter. Gennaro played out the net. We sat watching.

"How do you know when the fish come?"

"They jump out of the water."

I imagined them flinging themselves down on the deck in an ecstasy of surrender but nothing moved.

"Do they come for the insects or the light?"

Gennaro signed me to quiet. Perhaps they came for both, nourishment for body and spirit as the old preachers had it. Still nothing moved. Gennaro shrugged. I began to unbutton my shirt.

"What are you doing?"

"If there are no fish I'm going for a swim." I stood up and pulled off my shorts.

"You're mad. It's dangerous. There are big squid and rays; sharks, poisonous jellyfish."

"Not here." I pointed to the insect dance. "I'll be the only fish." I sat on the gunwale.

"Crazy! Don't do it. I'll go home and leave you."

"*Ciao!*" I slipped over the edge like the Little Mermaid turning into foam only there was none, just the warm saline bath and ripples of phosphorus that green fired off my body as I took a few leisurely strokes away from the boat. I almost choked with terror, trod water, and turned over on my back to float where I could watch the boat. The choking subsided. I was Osiris floating down the Nile in the sable chest that was my coffin while the beautiful Isis mourned along the bank for me. If I turned my head the other way the womb closed in; I began to panic under the padded darkness. Hastily I looked back at Gennaro. I must return. But I didn't want to. Out here I was complete and powerful as long as I could see the lights. By turning my head I could induce an orgasm of annihilation. I wanted this to go on and on, first one then the other; and there was the humiliation of clambering over the gunwale.

As I hesitated I felt a movement in the water that wasn't of my making. Gennaro's words of rays and jellyfish stung me. The suckered tentacles of the giant squid in the last reel of *Reap the Wild Wind* swaddled me with rubbery bands. Bile and brine filled my gullet but I kept quite still. Hundreds of little silver bodies were pushing past me, butting at my flesh and going on. When they brought in the drowned Shelley he was part nibbled away. Turning gently I flowed with them towards the boat, flung an arm over the side and stretched up a hand to Gennaro.

"Fish," I whispered, "thousands." At that moment the shoal rose like a wave crest through some pressure from below and broke in silver platelets.

"It's all wrong." He shook his head. The survivors swept on. "Help me." Slowly and carefully, afraid that it might break, we pulled the net on board until the bottom of the boat was full of little bodies jerking and skipping in a desperate bid for water. "That isn't how to catch fish."

"You should always use human bait." I had caused a miraculous draught of fishes; I was very pleased with myself. We shook the last live flashes out of the net. Gennaro pulled the starter.

"What are they?"

"Anchovies. Get dressed." He didn't know whether to be peeved or proud. The boat butted its way through the moist black velvet, heavier now with the twin lamps out. The smear of light gradually resolved into the Albergo; the light spar of the quay drifted out from the star-pricked cliff. We bumped against the concrete.

"What will you do?"

"I must fetch my father and a box to carry them in. When I have sold them I will give you half the money."

"I don't want it. Just some of the fish."

We took a winding lane through the cottages and off to the left, a part I'd never been in before, above the church where the ugly goddess reigned.

"There's no need . . ." Gennaro began but I caught hold of his arm. We were crossing the mouth of an alley that seemed to lead off the cliffside into nowhere; in fact a black silhouette of wall against the lighter darkness of sky endstopped it with a bastion from slipping down onto the beach.

"What's that?" A low but clear and insistent monotone came from the deep shadow by the wall.

"It's nothing."

I stepped softly into the mouth. There was a faint starshine now. A shape was hunched beside the wall, a man sitting on a box or stool alone. I listened carefully, but although the voice was almost at normal speaking level I still couldn't understand. Gennaro pulled me back. "What is it?" The voice went on, rising now as if some silent interrogater or interrogatee had objected or answered. "What's he doing?"

"Come away. He's cursing. Some trouble."

"What kind?"

"The family."

Sometimes as you passed the church there would be a man kneeling on the steps or prostrate like a kowtowing Oriental. If on his knees he would be bareheaded, his feet orderly together, and staring blank-eyed ahead towards the façade. He was always dressed in fisherman's best: a young man or a man in his prime performing a self-imposed penance on the hot stones. Maybe those on their faces were just at a later stage, fallen forward like scythed corn.

"We are passionate people. It's because we have Saracen blood. You are a child still. You don't understand anything. You must go back now."

"Can't I come with you?" I wanted to see Gennaro's home.

He sighed. "You are a child, see. You don't understand."

"What about my fish?"

"I will put some in a box for you."

"Alright. Meet me in the lane outside the garden."

"But . . ."

"Or I shall follow you now. I shall be at the bar," I added, "probably with the American girl."

"You are terrible. You are so old and so young both together. I will hide the fish beside the gate. Then I will come and tell you they are in place and take the American girl away."

"I don't want many. The rest are for you. See you." I turned and went back the way we'd come, a little frightened alone. The litany of malediction still fell monotonously out of the black alley mouth and I stopped a moment to listen. Maybe there was a set formula for such a rite, the opposite side of the silent penance on the church steps, an abracadabra handed down by the Turkish conquerors, which was why I couldn't understand it. Suddenly I thought I distinguished the standard word for to kill and a gush of the same fear I'd felt floating in the dark with my head turned away from the security of the lighted boat went through me and I crept away.

In the piazza bar I found the little group sitting as cozily as in the main street drugstore, though Gerry seemed a little low and looked up eagerly as the tail of her eye caught my entrance only to force a greeting when it was me. Had she already so attached herself to Gennaro like a young sea anemone on a host shellfish?

"Gennaro'll be along soon."

"Oh!" She was quick to cover her surprise that I'd caught her with her thoughts down. She began to wave her slender, brightest tendrils in anticipation.

"We've been out fishing."

"Oh!" I was glad to have reduced her conversation to monosyllables.

"You can buy me a drink. I haven't any money on me. I'll pay you back." I waved the waiter over. My mouth was very dry and salty from swimming and excitement. When I brushed a hand across my face it was gritty with dried brine. Snuffing the cupped palm I found it smelled as it did when I'd been caressing myself, only sharper. Maybe the sea is the gathered sweat of the land mixed with its tears. I was tired.

"Jon's coming back. I had a letter."

"Now what'll you do?"

"Geez I don't know. I mean I'm free and all that. Jon didn't surely expect me just to sit about. He might not have come. But I don't want him to think it's because . . . I don't know."

"Because he's black."

She looked shocked. "God, you're so, so blunt or do I mean sharp. Anyway . . . I guess I'll have to stick with Gennaro. I mean though he's not as clever or as educated as Jon he's awful sweet. And he'd be so hurt."

I could see she was enjoying the thought of the duel that might take place for her possession.

"I guess I just need somebody all the time. Isn't that awful to be so dependent."

"You're young and healthy."

"Sometimes you appal me. You think it's just sex.

You'd make me out some kind of nymphomaniac if you know what that means. You're so cold-blooded I can see the processes of evolution in you. You're still in the fish stage before they grew lungs and hearts and got themselves warm blood."

"You're angry with yourself," I said. She was hitting pretty hard and perhaps because I was tired I found a vulnerability in myself, a capacity to bruise. "You suspect you're maybe a nympho so you're lashing out at me. I'm tired of being told I don't understand just because I'm not sloppy and sticky. Who cares who you go to bed with. Who's best in bed anyway?"

"Gennaro," she said quickly and then, "I shouldn't have said that. Why do I talk to you as if you were an adult?"

"Cos I'm smarter than you."

"You know a lot of cheap psychology, *Reader's Digest* stuff. Well at least I don't insult Jon by pretending as if he wasn't a person."

"You mean the myth of the sexy Negro. What about the myth of the Latin lover?"

"My we are sharp this evening."

I leaned back and yawned. "I'm tired." I was giving myself away too much. The picture of Dorian Gray I keep locked in my own head must be being dangerously rejuvenated as I showed my wrinkles of worldly wisdom in public. Most people keep a mewling baby in themselves while they display an outward adult. I prefer it the other way round. Wearily I screwed my ingenuous smile into place. "I hope he comes soon."

"There he is now." She got up excitedly. Gennaro

nodded at me and waved to Gerry. She ran towards him and took his hand. There was a ripple of interest and approval from the fishermen's bar. Arturo, Gennaro's father, pushed his way forward through called greetings that I couldn't quite make out but were no doubt compliments on his son's double performance. I finished my drink, called to Leo that I'd bring him some fish in the morning, and walked home, retrieving the box from the bush beside the gate as I went in.

They were all gathered in the dining room still, chairs pushed back, relaxed. I thrust open the door, walked straight in and planted the box on the table. They lay there in their tight silver caul of new death, huddled together, each one quite perfectly cut from tin foil. They exuded a clean bright smell of sea like a pine deodorant. I felt a shock wave as I put them down and stood back but I didn't look at the faces. "I've been out catching breakfast."

"What are they?" asked Ajax.

"Anchovies."

"They look like sprats."

"Sprats?" my father queried.

"A sprat to catch a mackerel," my mother's lover explained. "A little silver fish like a sardine or these."

"They're very pretty," said my mother. "Poor things. Did you really catch them, darling?"

"I swam out to sea whistling them into my net. They like human bait." I knew no one would believe me but I had the release and excitement of telling a dangerous half-truth. "Gennaro came with me."

"The boy you used to play with?"

"We took his father's small boat."

"I thought you were meeting your American friend."

"I did. The signora can cook some of them for breakfast. Some I want to give to Leo."

"How do you cook them?" asked my mother, shielding herself from their small corpses and my drowning with a technical question.

"You toss them in flour and fry them," Ajax supplied.

"Strung together they'd make you a necklace. You could have a whole intricate design of them in rows like an Egyptian collar."

"Shouldn't they go into the fridge?" said Ajax, "to keep them really fresh. I'll take them if you like." My mother's lover wanted to remove the sight and smell of death from under her nose.

"I think I'll take a bath and some bed," I said. Ajax followed me out with the box.

When I'd turned the light out I lay afloat in my bed, my limbs as huge as Leviathan's, the attenuated trunk leading away, away from the experiencing head, waiting for the little mouths to butt against me until I became afraid and tried to get back my body by jerking off. But there was nothing there. Hard as I tried I was quite dead. I must have fallen asleep very suddenly.

In the morning the signora fried some of the fish for my father and me. With the rest I set out for Leo. "I thought you could do a Hemingway with them: the great outdoors; fish taken straight out of the lake and broiled in the glowing wood."

"Hell no; they're too small." He went into Honeymoon Hotel and came out with a battered skillet and a bottle of oil. Soon the smell of fried fish wafted out to sea. Leo ate them from the pan, burning his fingers, blowing on the fish and crunching them heads and all.

"Full of vitamins. You want some?"

"I already had some."

"Thought you'd just brought them along for me to do your cooking." One or two of the others drifted up and were given their share. I felt I was feeding the five thousand. In the end Leo wiped the pan clean of oil with some bread. "That's the best bit." He leaned back satisfied. "You're not a bad kid. I'll be moving on soon."

"Were you really in the Korean war?" He nodded. "Were you wounded?"

"They shot the balls off me. I was wounded in the spirit. That's the worst place they can hit you. I went in a boy and I came out an old man."

I smiled to myself in my old head. "But you don't mind taking the money?"

"I wouldn't go along with them even far enough to refuse it. Now I'm going to sleep some more. Just one big number and then I move on." Leo lay back on the sand with his head in the shade. I left him the box for firewood.

"That's coming very well," the Allthing was saying as I walked in. "I think a change of scene this afternoon."

"Where are you going?" I asked.

"Amalfi?" my mother questioned.

"Yes, that would be good. Not too far but something to look at when we get there."

"I'll stay home."

"Why, darling? Don't you feel well?"

"Sure. I'm fine. It's just that I've seen it and after all that fishing I might have a siesta," I joked.

"Would you like me to stay home with you?"

"Of course not. You could take Renata. I bet she's never seen the cathedral."

I waved them off: my father driving with Renata beside him; my mother and Ajax in back. Then I rang Gerry. "I'm coming up."

"Don't mind me. I wanted to do some shopping anyway."

"Good," I said cheerfully. "Just stay to let me in so I won't have to dare the little green men for once."

"The what?"

"Never mind."

"You know," she said when she'd closed the door, "you're the kind who gets written about in the papers. You get kids a bad name; you're a real junkie."

"Yeah, that's me."

"If I ever have children I'll be terrified since knowing you."

"Okay. You made your point. Now let me get to it."

"I don't know that I shouldn't tell someone about you."

"It's too late. Any way you look at it it's too late. Besides how would you look abetting me all this time? Suppose they sent me to a clinic or something, what good would that do? Maybe when I'm old enough to get really turned on by sex like you I'll kick the habit myself."

She slammed out, leaving me the key. For once there was no hurry. I savoured the ease of it. No one would interrupt me. I had all afternoon. In the bathroom I poured myself a glass of cold water and sipped it slowly, enjoying the conflict of my controlled movements, the cool deliberate trickle in the throat and the rising tension in my body as I strung myself on a taut wire of anticipation. Painstakingly I rinsed the glass and put it back above the washbasin, dried my hands, and went back into the bedroom.

The shutters pulled back easily, letting a surge of hot afternoon into the room. The glass doors were already open. I stepped onto the balcony. Every day now it grew a little hotter although one hardly noticed it, like the aging of a face seen daily. But on the balcony there was no respite of sea or shade. The fierce white light clanged as irresistibly as a steam hammer on the skin—into the mind through the shrivelling eyeballs. I remembered another late movie with Fantah where a soldier had been lost in the desert, his sight scorched out by the dazzle of the sands, the wheeling of vultures waiting for the charred remains to topple in a carrion heap. I think it was called *Four Feathers*. The sun was incandescent gas, Hiroshima cremating, Pompeii molten under lava. My head dizzied. The balcony wall burnt my hands as I climbed onto it. I had to grasp the drainpipe to steady myself. For a moment I thought I must let go but I clutched harder and deadened the pain with the pressure. Don't look down. I stretched a foot across the gap to Ajax' balcony, very aware that the space between my legs was about twenty feet deep, drew the other leg after it and shaking and pouring sweat lowered myself onto the tiled floor. For a reeling couple of seconds my body threatened to betray me in the vertigo of terror. The lack of reflection behind the shutters reassured me. The windows were open. I took out my pen-knife, opened the longest blade, and inserted it between the wooden uprights, sharpened edge uppermost, forcing it up against the metal bar that held them together until it was prised from its socket with a jerk. Quickly I withdrew the blade, closed and pocketed the knife, pulled the shutters towards me, and stepped into Ajax' room, fastening the shutters at my back.

Now I was here I wondered why I'd come. It was very cool and dim after the white heat outside. My shirt was soaked and clung to me coldly. I took it off, reopened the shutters; and stretched it out on the balcony. It would be dry in an instant. From the doorway while my shirt dried I studied the room. It was as tidy as ever giving me no clues as to my presence there. I turned back to my sweat-darkened shirt. The moisture had bleached out of it so rapidly you might have expected to see a visible steam rising from the cloth. I took it inside bone-dry and, closing both shutters and windows, hung it on a wooden chair-back. Then I took off my shorts and pants and stood quite naked, except for my sandals, in my mother's lover's bedroom. Bare feet would leave Man Friday footprints that might take time to dry. Though it didn't matter if Ajax knew someone had been there it was important that it should never be known who.

There was a box of Kleenex tissues on a dressing table. Taking one, I wiped the handles of window and shutters. Then I wrapped it round my fist like a bandage, opened the bathroom door and got a tooth glass, glancing up at the vent that looked as if it had never been meant to be covered. I took the scotch bottle from the other dressing table where I had seen Ajax take it from and, with another tissue for the left hand as well, poured myself a drink. The fiery honey-coloured spirit stung my mouth. The second gulp I held, swilling it against my tongue and teeth before I could swallow it. The sudden flame in my belly broke me into sweat again. I felt marvellous. I wondered if I should quietly wreck the room but that seemed too crude. I would be more subtle. I began to open all the drawers and doors, systematically. About me hung that same faint perfume I'd noticed before. Now I was sure it was my mother's. It was almost as if she was present watching me. Almost. I took another gulp of the whisky.

The letters were in the cheap suitcase in the second wardrobe. There had been nothing else except the clothes I was used to seeing on Ajax, few of them and all put tidily in appropriate piles. The letters were in my mother's unmistakeably beautiful hand, three of them, all written since I'd come back, the most recent only the day before yesterday. They were quite simply effusions of love. I read them all. "I am so happy with you. Believe that I love you," said the last. I put it in my shorts pocket. It made me want to cry and laugh at the same time. The rest of the scotch went down in one swallow. Once you had the taste for it it was easy.

Drowsy, heavy-limbed, I lay down on the bed I had watched through the periscope. My mind had no doubts now about that perfume. It was as if I had sunk deep into a flower, a white peony. Lust had impregnated the sheets on my mother's lover's bed with her balm. At night Ajax could sink again into her flesh. And I lay there as naked as either of them, playing first one and then the other as I'd seen them. Now when my mother's lover lay down it would be into a mingling of my sweat with theirs. When I came it was so hard and fierce I thought I was going to be sick but that may have been the unaccustomed scotch in my stomach.

I felt strong but empty and got up at once and went into the bathroom where I washed myself and the used tumbler. It was time to go. First I must smooth the bed and put my clothes on. Wearing my tissue bandages, I opened the french doors. One more look around to make sure all was as I'd found it before I let myself cautiously out into the corridor, shut the door, and stuffed the tissues into the pocket with the letter and went downstairs swinging Gerry's key, which I left at the desk. Back in the safety of my room I hid tissues and letter in my pillowcase, glad for once that my mother believes everyone should make his own bed. My legs ached and I longed for sleep but I crossed the landing to my parents' room.

In the writing desk in a corner I knew I should find my mother's distinctive lilac writing paper and envelopes. I took one specimen of each, noted the kind of ink bought locally and was back in my own bed in three minutes. I timed it.

I'd never practised forgery before. Ink and a selection of nibs I bought in the square and smuggled up to my room. It amused me to ask Ajax for some sheets of top copy to practise on. I'd bought some blotting paper too, principally to slip over what I was doing if anyone should come in. My protohero Master Krull had found it quite easy. He'd become proficient enough at signatures to fool banks and eventually at a whole script to fool parents. I was disappointed in myself that I found it so hard even though I wasn't aiming at such a standard of excellence. I only needed to be able to con the eye of a lover. Surely that was easier. Haven't we always been told that the lover sees evidence of the beloved everywhere? The very colour of the envelope should be suggestive to Ajax.

At first I simply traced whole words several times to accustom myself to the shapes. Then I began to wonder whether it should be a purely mechanical activity like the decipherment of an ancient script or whether I would do better to Stanislavski myself into the role. Felix had been able to use a little of both: he had after all only been in the forgery business as a byproduct of his total impersonation as well as having great technical, or do I mean manual, skill. He could even draw pictures in the style of. Had Van Meegeren thought himself into Vermeer? Had he thought the strokes on the canvas were Vermeer's, perhaps even the hands as he watched them moving? How far in did the impersonation go? And Chatterton? Had he in the act of enditing heard his own time grow fainter outside the garret window to be replaced by the clash of chivalry? Wasn't he born out of his time? The forger was very close to the restorer and translator but just the wrong side of the accepted line. You could get away with it in architecture. As long as you were in the style of without pretending you were the person. Yet you had to pretend to that a bit, I was sure of it now, if you wanted to be successful. Perhaps that was really what forgers were punished for: usurpation, a blurring of the lines between two people. It was always some third party that objected: the state, the buyer, the critic. Young Chatterton was undoubtedly a genius. He *was* Thomas Rowley, monk.

But who was I impersonating? No wonder I found it so hard. It's true that I'm also some kind of monster-genius but my mother is perfection, apart from that Achilles heel of believing herself in love. She must be allowed some human weakness. I was impersonating her at her weakest in a letter to her lover. I ran through phrases in my head. What would the loving I say to Ajax? I tried a sentence or two on the smooth white sheet. It looked pretty good and I was pleased with it as a work of art but it wouldn't fool anyone. Love was surprisingly hard to simulate. The highest flights of forgery are close to creation: another reason for its being execrated. Though would-be censors claim art is a- or im-moral, in fact they rely all the time on the real morality of art, its self-integrity. Forgery has none because it has no self. It's truly, audaciously, disorderingly immoral. I was very excited. I seemed to be breathing heady bubbles of anarchy like laughing gas. I could be my mother in an act of verbal love and with a flick of the pen, a word in here, I could negate it, mock, erupt into obscenity in her own hand.

However I must calm myself and be careful. The exhilaration of the artist must give way to the cool appraisal of the man of affairs. To make love to Ajax by proxy wasn't the answer. Anything so unsubtle would lead straight to me as the only possible author. There was no amusement in being caught. The game was for the playing's sake; not to be won or lost. I studied the bonanza, the letter, I'd gained and tried to figure how to lay it out for the greatest possible return. It was nearly lunchtime. I put my materials safely away, washed up, and went downstairs on rubbersoled feet. At the dining room door I paused. It wasn't quite shut. There were voices. I don't believe in missing an opportunity.

"That last letter you sent me . . ."

"Yes?"

"It's gone. I thought I'd put it in the case with the others. Last night I went to get it to read in bed."

"Darling."

"It wasn't there. The other two were but not that one."

"Are you sure you put it in there, darling?"

"I thought I was."

"Perhaps it's somewhere else; in a pocket . . . ?"

"I did carry it about with me at first. Then I thought it'd be safer . . ."

"Perhaps you only intended to and then thought you had. Don't worry about it. It's probably still in a pocket."

"I suppose so. It's funny: you make it seem alright but last night I was quite convinced someone had been into my room and taken it."

"What made you think so?"

"That's it, you see. I can't pinpoint it. Only last night I was sure of it when I couldn't find your letter. I thought the windows were different and the coverlet on the bed."

"The maid?"

"Could be. You know what it's like at night. Everything magnified. It seemed as if I'd lost you too and then myself."

"Oh my dear! You haven't, you see. Even if the letter's gone it doesn't mean anything."

"It's not so much that anyone should find it; it's the loss. It was very precious to me."

"Past tense?"

Ajax laughed. "I'm sorry."

Silently I retreated upstairs again. Sometimes it doesn't do to come jump upon one's cue. The combination of two images may give rise to a third by some natural process in the mind without anyone having to put two and two together. I didn't go down til I heard from my listening post at the head of the stairs that my father had joined them. By the same fecund process their conversation had caused ideas to sprout in my head. I knew now what I should write and it was so marvellously simple it filled me with admiration.

By an extraordinary piece of luck it seemed, or so my mother told me when she came to say goodnight, that I should have just the chance I wanted to try out my skill as a forger. My parents were going to lunch next day with a NATO acquaintance of my father's in Naples. Ajax and I would be alone. I could hardly sleep for the joyful anticipation. I read her letter through a couple of times. I knew it by heart of course, but the object itself was so much a part of her that it wasn't the same merely to repeat the words in one's head. After, I slept with it inside my pillowcase again where I could hear it rustle slightly. It was clear from the definition of the folds that Ajax had already read it many times before me. It bore the imprint of veneration, the slightly tawdry rubbed look of a cult object.

I stood in the shadows at the top of the stairs again in the morning. My father was already in the car. Ajax had come early. I was feigning sleep.

"You know I don't like to leave you even for half a day. Don't let Kit chase about in the sun too much. I'll be back as soon as I can, darling." There was a pause. I pressed hard back against the wall lest crossing to the car she should look up and see me through the upper windows. The engine roared. The door closed. I tiptoed back to my room to prepare my masterpiece.

By the time I came down I could hear the rumble of the tape recorder and the chatter of the typewriter. I fixed myself some coffee and a roll and went through into the dining room. Ajax looked up and grinned. I put a finger to my lips and motioned for the work to go on. I settled myself down to listen. The tape was halfway through. My mother's lover seemed to be making a transcript of it or maybe an edited version.

"Can we say then that determinism is a new doctrine based on accumulated scientific and psychological data?" my father said.

"A refurbished doctrine." My mother's voice. "Isn't the idea of fate the same thing in mythological form?"

"Both gods and men were under the fates, weren't they? Only Zeus as father figure was sometimes almost exempt, which makes good psychological sense." Ajax.

"How?"

"Well, one's father is generally thought or felt to be all-powerful and he seems to control his children's fate."

"Yes, that would seem to be it. Why then are the fates always women?"

"Because it's the mother who controls one's birth and therefore death." My mother.

"Good, good. Originally the Norns were only one, Urd, representing the past. They became three by analogy with the Parcae." My father.

"Was the idea then that the past rules men's lives? That'd seem a form of determinism."

"Then there's the fatalism of Greek drama. Everything is done to prevent Oedipus killing his father and marrying his mother but he is unable to escape his laid-down fate." My mother.

"Which would suggest . . . ?"

"An immutable in-built psychological law." Ajax.

"Free will is the new concept introduced by Christianity: that we can govern our fate by free moral choices. Existentialism is Neo-Christianity."

"Protestant insistence on predestination would seem to be a return to fatalism." My father.

"We are on a constant seesaw between the two. Is that because though rationally we know about causation and determinism we behave as if there were free will as a product of the biological instincts for self-preservation and reproduction? Unless one acts life can't continue, yet the pattern of its continuance is already laid down. So two seemingly contradictory ideas have to be held in synthesis." Ajax.

"How can you stop the pattern?"

"By choosing not to go on."

"The illusion of free will. Yet even that's determined by a set course of events and by your own genetic and environmental conditioning." My mother.

"I think I need to believe that I have that freedom in order not to get claustrophobia."

"Did Oedipus get claustrophobia?" My mother.

"Isn't that why he blinded himself—that is, made himself impotent as a protest against, which is also a succumbing to, causation and the closed world."

"Gestures are empty?" My father.

"Sometimes gestures are all we have left. They may be very beautiful."

"And to stop the pain. It may be better for a caged animal to beat itself to death." Ajax.

"Than to be given a hypodermic and conditioned into acceptance."

"So a tenable view of life would seem to be like a wildlife reserve, where one lives in pre-set conditions with an illusion of freedom: neither the jungle of free will nor the zoo of unrelieved determinism. Life as we think we know it is an illusion we create, like art." My father.

"And the riddle of the Sphinx?" Ajax.

"A schoolboy's question and answer about the nature of man that allays our fears and lets us do what we want to do, which is what we are programmed to want."

My mother's voice ceased and Ajax switched off the tape recorder.

"That was some discussion. What were you high flying on? Where is everybody anyway?"

"They're out to lunch."

I whistled. "Yeah, I remember now. Oh well . . ."

"Did you want something in particular?"

"It's just I found this letter of mother's in a book. She

must have slipped it in and forgotten to post it." I held out the lilac envelope so that Ajax could read the name and address. "It's got a stamp on it so I'll just drop it in on my way down." I slipped it into my pocket.

"You're going out?"

"Just down to the shops. I need a couple of things. I'll be back for lunch." I swung out with a cheerful whistle.

In the square I met Gerry, the Indian sandals brave but battered now, her face sulky. "I need someone to talk to and there's only you."

"Thank you very much."

"I'll buy you a drink."

"Now who's desperate?"

Her eyes filled with tears. "I don't get any nearer finding myself. Why doesn't it trouble you? You're a worse mess than I am. Or maybe you're not and that's it."

"Tell junior," I said, afraid she was going to rain all over the table.

"Jon's back."

"How is he?"

"He's fine, just fine."

"So?"

"You know I told you about this rich old musician in Paris who gives him money?" I nodded. "Well, when he heard Jon had been here he gives him an introduction to some famous singer who lives here and as soon as Jon turns up she snaps him off the doormat quicker than you can say welcome. What's more her boyfriend who lives there too doesn't seem to mind a bit."

"He's not her boyfriend."

"How would you know?"

"He's just one of her conductors. They're friends of my parents. I can see Ellie would like Jon."

"She made him move in with just a bedding roll and she's bought him some new clothes and the kids just love him. And I'm the most godawful person in the world."

"And how's Gennaro?"

"He's so sweet and I'm such a shit. He's too good for me."

"I thought that was Jon."

"I guess basically I just feel everyone's too good for me."

"Or not good enough."

"Oh trust you to come out with the textbook answer. Alright so I'm a megalomaniac."

"Stop worrying. Enjoy yourself."

"That's what Leo says. I guess he's the only wise man I'm ever likely to meet up with."

"Well I have to go. Shall I give Jon your love?"

She looked at me sharply. "Why do you say that?"

"I think I'll look in on Ellie."

"Oh you're so busy. I don't care what you say. Sometimes you seem to me like some spiteful, elderly cupid played by a dwarf instead of a child."

"A 'shrewd and knavish sprite.'" I got up. "Thanks for the drink."

"You can give Jon my love."

"Whatever that means. Will do. See you."

Ellie's villa lies to the right, a little apart among trees and shrubs of every kind the place will grow but particularly oleander and bougainvillaea, which somehow seem imported there from some set for a Southern belle opera with chorus of crooning old-time coons, Delius' unwritten American *Eugene Onegin*. We wait now for the musical version of *All This and Heaven Too*. Indeed when Ellie sang Olga once there was more than a touch of Scarlett O'Hara about her. She wonders why she's never been asked to do Tatyana now her voice has gone up. So the villa itself seems somehow set beside the old bayou and Ellie at home inclines to white sprigged muslin. Jon's presence must give her an added frisson. I expected to hear a slight drawl to her voice. Architecturally the native has triumphed. It's the largest of the villas but modern with a dash of Spanish in its outer wall pierced by a rounded arch. Ellie often laments that it isn't more "colonial," which she derives from "Colonel." There's a walled courtyard with a fountain and twisted sugar-candy columns like a Moorish cloister. They were all three gathered there: Caspar dark as an Indian on an inflated mattress, Ellie swinging and fanning herself in a hammock under an awning, Jon in crisp new shirt and pants tumbling with the children. I thought of Mardian and hoped there was enough bull in him.

"Why, Kit, how nice," Ellie purred from the hammock.

"Hi man!" I said to Jon. I was glad to see she hadn't got him into shorts yet.

"Hi!"

"Gerry sends her love."

He smiled. Ellie straightened in the hammock and lowered her feet to the floor. Caspar opened an eye. I sat on the ground leaning back on straight arms.

"The family sends its communal regards. You owe us a visit."

"I know but it's so hot and I'm so lazy."

"How's your mother?" Caspar asked.

"She's fine. A bit bored but then who isn't in this place. You should give a party, Ellie."

"I'm so lazy."

"Leo's moving on soon," I said to Jon. "He's talking of a big number before he goes."

"Who's Leo?" Ellie asked sleepily.

"A friend of mine," Jon said. He had stopped playing with the children or they, seeing a change in mood, had moved away from him.

"You seem to know a lot of people here."

"Why not give a party for Leo before he goes."

Jon looked at Ellie. "Maybe he wouldn't want to come up here."

"He'll go wherever there's a free drink."

"Why not," said Caspar.

"Oh alright. As long as I don't have to do anything. It's too hot," Ellie fanned.

"You'll just have to look beautiful," said Caspar.

"Maybe you could sing," Jon suggested, a little wistfully.

"As long as I don't have to write any invitations or cook."

"When have you ever cooked?" Caspar laughed. "We'll do all that."

"If you wrote a note to mother now I could take it back with me."

"*Hélas.*" Caspar slithered to his feet and went inside to re-emerge with pen and card. "What date shall I make it?"

"The day after tomorrow?" Everyone nodded. "I leave you to invite Gerry. You'd better ask her boyfriend too." I took the card from Caspar. "See you *dopodomani.*" On the way home I matched Caspar's ink and nib. I was really getting quite a repertoire.

At lunch I told Ajax all about St. Gelbert's and about Fantah. I had to go back into the past and to unfamiliar territory for topics since the present and familiar was so loaded it seemed as untouchable as an antipersonnel bomb with a trembler fuse. In return I got a chunk of Ajax' childhood.

"Come up to my room and I'll show you something I've made." My mother's lover followed me up the stairs. "Sit on the bed." I wanted Ajax in my room; I wanted to walk this particular ironical highwire.

"Look."

"It's a periscope, isn't it?"

"That's right."

"What's it for?"

"I just wanted to see if I could; if it would work." I wanted Ajax' praise.

"Can I try it?"

"Sure. Try it out of the window."

"I can't . . . Yes, I can. I can almost see what's happening round the corner of the house. It's very clear. Like a small photograph." Ajax sat down on the bed again; one hand outstretched could have touched the letter. "I must get back to my work. What are you going to do?"

"Some Latin I think."

"What have you got to now?"

"Apollo and Daphne. She was a silly girl. Why didn't she simply lie back and enjoy it? What's the good of just getting in poets' hair for the rest of your immortal life."

Ajax laughed, letting the tension out of the moment.

"And, after all, Apollo was quite some catch."

My mother's lover stood up. Did I hear the letter cry out with its rustled protest? I was reminded suddenly by a trick of the afternoon sun through the unshuttered windows of the first time I'd seen Ajax balancing in a pool of purple light.

I set to work on Caspar's script, easier than my mother's because of its foreign floridness.

"So you are *ennuyée*," he had written, "with the pleasures of this sultry paradise. Allow me to divert you. We are giving a party. You will not be bored. Ellie will sing and you must steel yourself to be enraptured. Jon promises many of his old friends as appetizers.

Yours,
Caspar"

It was only a matter of a little judicious insertion. The fates had been good, as they say, and Caspar's flourishes left gaps in the most likely places. After study and practice I put in a "by me" after "bored," altered the "steel" to "steal," adding an "away by" immediately. "Yours" I embellished with "ever." Caspar would have been deceived by his own fluency. The last sentence took on a quite new meaning. I really felt the whole thing showed a genius for de-composition. I sealed it in an envelope and superscribed my mother's name. Shown it I doubted whether Caspar himself would have remembered precisely enough what he'd written to disown it.

I heard them come back but stayed in my room until dinner, when I knew everyone would be assembled.

"I was up at Ellie's today. Caspar gave me this for you." My mother took it smiling. "One of my friends from the beach has moved in with Ellie." She was reading the missive; the smile turned to a look of annoyance. "He's a composer. Apparently some old musician in Paris gave him an introduction. Ellie took one look and snapped him up."

"He must have been drunk when he wrote this." As if absentmindedly she tore the card in four and put it back in the envelope. "What's it supposed to be about? He says a party."

"That's right. Ellie's giving a party for Jon, the one I was telling you about, or for Jon's friends. I'm not sure quite which. You know how they are up there. Anyway we're all to go the day after tomorrow."

"I suppose we must."

"We must take Renata. It'll give her a chance to meet the boums," I said.

"What does Caspar say?" My father was curious.

"I can't really make sense of it. He must have been drunk."

"Too early in the day."

"Heat stroke then. Shall we have a drink before dinner? The trouble with lunching out is that you start drinking too early and then you have to keep topped up in order not to sink into a post-alcoholic depression. Would you like to give me a Punt e Mes?" She smiled at Ajax, who bowed a little. "I've come down without a handkerchief too; I must just go up and get one." She left the room. I could hardly refrain from applause and reflected that perhaps more of my gifts than I'd thought were inherited. She was only gone a few moments but she had left the envelope behind. How would she play the next round?

"Ellie's going to sing." Very cool. "Is that for me?" She took her drink from her lover's outstretched hand. Oh my mother you are a queen in a house of knaves; I would not challenge you. Neither will your lover. The signora brought in a steaming bowl of pasta, butterflies bloodied with ketchup of *sugo al pomidoro*.

"Shall we ask Renata?" My father scraped out his chair.

"I'm sure the feeling was the more the merrier. Ellie's such a folksy thing at heart she's never got beyond square dancing: change partners when the caller says so. 'It's the latest thing in Utah, ma'am,' he said, aiming a long squirt of fluoride-anti-carries-your-personal-guarantee gum juice accurately at a Cola can and hitching his bermudas."

"You have a very good line in fantasy, darling."

"Will the signora have to go too as chaperone?" Ajax asked.

"No chaperones," I said. " 'I tell thee they have made me mad.' Maybe we could fix her up with someone."

"And what about you?" said my father.

" 'Young I am and yet unskill'd.' My trouble is I can't choose between Gennaro and Gerry. I think basically I just think I want everybody and don't really want anybody." I said it feigning honesty so that it should be thought a cover but it was true. It was a trick I'd learned from watching politicians on television at election time. If a candidate said he was himself indifferent honest but he could accuse himself of such things it was better his mother had not borne him, or that he was only human, had all the same faults as any other manjack, then the audience would assume he was covering up a great virtue. Admit your vices with a show of frankness and they won't be believed. "Leo will probably sing too."

"It will be all mosquitoes and assorted *bestuoli*," said my mother. "Ugh, how I hate the great outdoors. Perhaps it'll rain."

"A fierce operatic storm to send us all scurrying in." I waved my fork like a baton. Ajax seemed unusually quiet; my father in good spirits. I guessed the book was going well. The exercise of power in the form of advice to the nations confirms his own strength as well as that he leeches from his young companions in arms. He is really happy when he is swinging some theoretical double axe and the hordes are falling back before him.

The moment I'd been hoping for came when I'd almost despaired of it after dinner. My father went to the john, my mother to get a fresh pack of cigarettes. The signora was clearing the dishes.

"Personally," I said to Ajax, "I think Caspar stage-managed the whole thing. He's so gone on mother." I said it with perfect childlike innocence not knowing I was addressing my mother's lover but only my father's secretary, who was just like one of the family.

"Maybe it will rain," Ajax made the effort.

"Oh it never rains here in the summer."

For the rest of the evening Ajax was dumb, speaking only out of some social compulsion, the words dragged up from the pit and clothed in a false brightness that might deceive my father but no one else. Unconcerned I chattered on, though my mother was often abstracted too. My father gave us an account of the lunch and the workings of UNICEF. Ajax got up to go early. There'd been no move towards the bar. I'd sat my mother's lover out. I gave them no chance to speak, accompanying my mother to the front door for waved goodnights.

"I think I'll go to bed too." I yawned. I had to partly undress in case my mother should come in to see me. I heard them come upstairs and pass the door. My light was out. In a few moments there was the sound of their door opening and then my own.

"Goodnight, darling."

I made a sleepy noise that was half grunt. The wedge of light went away; the door shut softly. At once I was out of bed redressing in the dark. Hooking Gennaro's grappling iron over the window sill I scrambled down the rope, ran silently up the garden and out of the gate, taking the stick bolt with me and pulling the door into place. The hot night crackled with insect life as I hurried through it. There was no precise expectation in my mind, only an urge to watch and see. This time I felt no fear in the dark lanes. Ribbed oblongs of light showed side by side from Gerry's and Ajax' windows like an X ray of some monster robot chest cavity. There was no grey on black abstract of a signal towel over the balcony.

The receptionist smiled and rang Gerry. "She says to

go up." This was the worst part of all. I ran up the staircase, ignoring the lift, and flattened myself round the corner where I could peer down the corridor. Suppose Ajax were to come out now on the way to the bar? It was only ten thirty. If I waited a moment or two Gerry might get impatient and step out to look for me. I heard a door opening. Her head appeared, turning to left and then right. I ran tiptoe towards her, a finger on my lips, expressive and as graceful and soundless, I hoped, as ever Nijinsky was. Her mouth was open to speak as she saw me. It stayed open in amazement as I flapped at her to be quiet. Then we were inside and I clicked the door gently behind us.

"I thought I saw someone we know. I didn't want to be caught in the open. I'm supposed to be in bed." I whispered as if it was church.

"If you could have seen youself flitting along waving your arms like some . . ."

"Old faggot."

"You shouldn't know about such things. I don't hardly."

"I was born older than you and in my home there's free discussion on all topics."

"Look where it's gotten them," she hissed. As I'd hoped my lowered tones were infectious but it made us members of some vaudeville act taking a stab at each other between toothily smiling curtain calls. "What's that?" She pointed to the periscope in my hand. "I thought for a crazy moment you'd gone berserk and were going to take a swing at me with it."

"It's a piece of my equipment."

"What's it . . . ? No, I don't want to know. Geez, you terrify me."

"I use it to intensify the experience. I . . ."

She put up a hand. "I definitely don't want to know. In fact I'm going out so I'm not quite party to whatever you get up to."

" '. . . madam. I can do nothing.' " I gave a little Ajax bow.

> " 'Yet have I fierce affections, and think
> What Venus did with Mars.' "

"That has to be Shakespeare. You're too bright and too literate. Ill weeds or something." There was a sound from next door. "Now the neighbours are getting noisy."

"Go down to the square. Maybe all the old gang'll be there. Jon wants to see you, by the way. He's got some kind of invitation for you."

"Just leave the key at the desk."

Inside the bathroom I bolted the door. The cardboard of the periscope showed wet indentations where I'd had to hold it in my mouth to climb down the rope. I was trembling with an excitement I hoped wouldn't make me clumsy as I mounted the john and removed the vents. Gently I inserted the periscope and then withdrew it hastily but silently, got down and put off the light before I took up my position again, staring through the little tunnel with naked eye. The lights were all on and Ajax was framed perfectly by the square. There was no need to see to the far bed. I was looking through the little door into the inaccessible garden where my mother's lover raged and wept like some inhabitant of Dante's hell. I hadn't known what I expected, but not Prometheus under the eagle, chained to the cliff, or Lucifer to the burning lake. Ajax had been drinking. The near empty bottle of scotch stood on the floor. One hand gripped the glass, the other was splayed over the face that was wet with tears and screwed up into a fist of misery. Ajax moaned and the free hand beat with the heel of the palm against the broad forehead. The glass was emptied and set down. My mother's lover got up wildly, hands clawing at the face. For a moment I thought it might be Oedipus self-blinded —I was quite cold observing every detail—but the figure stumbled out of my vision. Then, though I couldn't see, I knew that Ajax was beating on the wall. I heard the blows and cries, fists of anguish that thudded into my own head. This was what I had read about and now I'd caused it to happen in a long ejaculation of grief. Now I knew more about my mother's lover than she did because I'd seen Ajax as an omniscient might see when one is alone and not even acting for oneself. It was maybe more indecent to go on watching than if one had been eavesdropping on an act of pleasure.

Back in my bed I thought it was right that Ajax should go down into hell for my mother. It fitted. The cries had ceased, had become sobs. I had put back the vent, hidden the periscope, and left.

The next day, gentle reader, passed quietly enough, Ajax being very subdued, overhung with an excess of liquor and passion. I carried Ellie's invitation to Leo in case it shouldn't have reached that far yet. "Will you come?"

"It's free drink? Then I'll come."

"You don't mind taking from the rich."

"And giving to the poor? I've told you before, man, you mustn't even ride along with them far enough to accept their money morality."

"Bring your guitar."

"So's I can sing for my supper? They put a price on everything."

I don't remember now the intervening hours I was so high on anticipation, and in between my trips of euphoria I slept as if I'd been running for miles. Suddenly, it seemed, we were all dressing for the party. We ate at the pizzeria, the rest drinking themselves into a false gaiety while I needed only a mouthful which I insisted on taking from my mother's glass to set me humming and spinning.

Oh *fêtes ungalantes, bale de champêtre*, I have created you. I am forger and impresario, artist of the truly pop, whose subjects are four-dimensional, breathing, my puppets, my pieces, I ringmaster. I am the Great Stromboli jerking your strings and, like him, when I've done with you I destroy you. For me you trot in time and leap through hoops of fire however much you may rage and try to defy me. I have made a work of fleshly humans as if they were waxworks in a tableau.

When you have nothing but craft you must create in the round, a happening, a ritual like the great hysterias of the past—the revivalist meetings of sin, blood, and penitence, the crusades of violence, the witchings, executions in the marketplace, riot and hunger march, the loosing of the black Dionysus in Saturnalia.

In an age when the passions were still there just

below the surface, refined and held in place by reason, the crust on the bubbling molten core, the rite could be civilized in the *bal masqué,* a beaked, peaked cover, licence to act out. Now we go masked all the time wearing our own set faces over nothing. Invite us to the Bacchanal and we laugh with embarrassment, Pentheus everyone for whom the fawnskin and the twined thyrsis are merely ridiculous. It's not that we won't dance; we can't.

But I have made a public spectacle, a piece of art as ephemeral as an evening and never to be repeated. I have stolen the world's most beautiful painting and hung it in my own head for my exclusive pleasure. Puckily I scurried here and there among my actors, provoking them into audience participation, a wilful anarchic act of creation from the spirit of the times: let us see what would happen. For when you are making your own myth you can't know its end. I tell you I didn't know.

What ho, what ho! Welcome to the Island of Cythera. Ellie's estate is hung with lamps: an islet of light adrift in a night sea.

"You're very charming tonight, Kit."

"Would you seduce me, Ellie?

'Take me, take me some of you,
While I yet am young and true.' "

"My the child does go on. The garden's full of strange people. I suppose they're all friends of Jon's. I never knew there were so many U.S. emigrés in this little place. Help yourselves to drinks. Caspar's somewhere by the bar."

Under the trees figures recline or swim blurrily in the

lamplight. I have brought the goddess to preside over the revels but not to stand enshrined before the fountain her lover. She too shall take part.

"This way, this way!"

"Where are we going?"

"I want you to meet Leo."

"But the drinks?"

"Caspar will see to them. Look, there's Gerry. You must meet Gerry. Doesn't mother look fabulous this evening! No wonder everyone falls for her. Gerry, this is Ajax. Have you got a drink? I'll bring them. Stay right there."

So I push and pull, loosing now the lead tip, now the silver, smiling cherubically. Lead on the rout. Renata and her mother are trotting in double harness through the archways as if down the aisle to a bridal altar, the signora in fuchsia shot with sequins, her daughter virginal under the purring cat face. Ellie will be angry, out-hymened in her own backyard; my father amusedly flattered as they play each other for suckers.

"I've introduced Ajax and Gerry. They're getting on splendidly. I'll take them a bottle and a couple of glasses. Are you going to have to play barman all evening?"

"I hope Ellie will let me off long enough for at least one turn round the estate with your mother."

"You're looking very beautiful this evening, maman, isn't she, Caspar?"

"In this light it's difficult not to be deceptive." This isn't false modesty: she has no idea of her own goddesship. "I must circulate. Introduce me to some of your friends." She smiles charmingly but with slightly lowered voltage at Caspar. We drift away like unanchored seaweed through deep placid waters. Venus isn't self-regarding. If she looks at herself in the mirror it is only to see what her lover sees and to embellish for her lover's pleasure. Mostly she doesn't look.

"Maman, this is Gerry. What happened to Ajax?"

"Took off to find some drinks or someone."

"I've brought the drinks."

"Have you seen Jon?"

"Ellie's keeping him under cover. Where's Gennaro?"

"He said he'd be along. Can I have some of that?"

"Sure. Maman?"

"Thank you, darling. I think I'd better find your father. I expect I'll see you both later."

But she has gone to look for Ajax while Ajax is seeking her among the oleanders. Under Ellie's lamps their flowers are cut from tissue paper; in the shadows they are moulded in wax. Ellie herself reappears from the archway of the walled courtyard, leaning on Jon's arm. She has dressed him in white and silver brocade.

"Look at that old woman, Kit, how she hangs on him."

" 'Like a rich jewel in an Ethiope's ear.' "

"Haven't you any words of your own?"

"All the words have been said and anyway I'm too young."

"She's every crease of forty-five."

"Ellie's a star and a business woman. Like my father she needs to be nourished at the fountain of youth. One day she won't be able to hit the high notes so she has an insurance: Friedland Frosco." I am quoting table talk.

"She's Friedland's Frosco?" I nod. "All those shiny metal containers and deep freezes the size of an apartment block at every railroad depot, the wharves you see as the ship pulls out?" I nod again. "Then why?"

"Black power." I whisper. "Here's Gennaro." Gerry turns and sees his hands full of sponges and fish scales powdering his hair like Christmas frost.

"*Ciao, tritonino.*"

"What did you call him?"

"Merboy."

"*Cosa?*"

"You must be strong with her. The moon has made her a little mad tonight." I skip behind a bush.

He takes both her hands and throws a net over her with his eyes. "*Cara!*" She flounders. Her limbs turn to water.

The bush smells honey and warm. I'm reminded of my task. The signora and my mother are pacing towards me.

"The garden is very beautiful. Shall we go into the courtyard? Have you seen the villa?"

"Yes. I've been here twice before. Madam was ill. Someone had recommended me. The garden was not so beautiful. It was winter."

"And the second time?"

"The next day. It was very cold."

They passed through the archway. There was a tinkle from the fountain where Ellie's snowchild played in unopened bud. The basin had been sprinkled with white petals that swam in the plashes like swanboats.

"Who is that so handsome tall man, very dark?"

"That's Caspar."

"Caspar?"

"Caspar Melchitz, the conductor."

"He is famous?"

"Very. Where's my father?"

"He is with the boums. Why is he?"

"He is trying to pick their brains."

"What is that?"

"To understand them for his book."

"Oh. There are many important people here?"

"Some friends of Ellie's. Here's Caspar. I'll introduce you. Signorina Gambardella, Signor Melchitz."

"*Piacere.* Ellie's going to sing now. Shall we go into the courtyard?"

From all sides they are converging on the square through the shadows of the garden, the voices rising up through the evening like the cries of unseen birds. A piano stands on the flagstones where we reclined. Light drains out of the house to be sopped up by swagged drapery of darkness. Jon is at the piano. The fountain accompanies him modestly.

"What will she sing?"

" 'Tu, tu piccolo Iddio' from *Madama Butterfly.*"

"I have seen. It is very beautiful. There is my mother."

"And mine."

"It is the last moment before she kills herself, with the baby, isn't it?"

Ajax is at the other side of the courtyard from my mother and the signora. My mother's lover sees her, turns to go out through the arch, but other people are pressing in and at this moment Ellie enters from the house carrying Butterfly's white scarf. Jon strokes the keys to crescendo.

"Shhh! shhh!"

" 'Tu, tu, tu, tu . . .' "

The child listens by the fountain. Ellie is magnificent. Are there two small white smudges at an upper window?

" '*Addio! piccolo amor! Va. Gioca.*' "

The human voice stills. Under Jon's fingers she binds the child's eyes and puts the American flag and a toy in its hands. The dagger falls from a crashing chord. Ellie's hand sinks on her breast.

Applause, applause.

Ajax is gone. My mother and the signora start towards us past the fountain. Jon closes the piano and leads Ellie to join us.

"You were marvellous."

"Quite the best I've heard you this year."

"It's too much. It shouldn't really be shown on the public stage. I always weep."

"It is very beautiful."

More wine, more wine. Caspar is Dionysus who will pour unending chalices to seal our communion.

"Are you alright, darling?"

"Yes, my tactful maman."

"Have you see Ajax? I thought . . ."

"Just before Ellie sang."

"Here's your rival, Ellie."

Leo is bearing his guitar like a slung child at his breast into the limelight.

"Do wé have to? It'll go on and on I know."

"Yes, we have to."

She pouts a little but Jon is firm. The disciples have pressed forward. I see Ajax at the back of the crowd where my mother had stood; and Gerry, mouth a little open, holding Gennaro's hand. Leo plants one foot on the edge of the fountain, plucks a few thin strings, begins a thrumming continuous Niagara of chords.

> " 'Carl Solomon! I'm with you in Rockland
>   where you're madder than I am . . .' "

"What is it?"

My father has come up to stand with us. "It's a poem by Allen Ginsberg."

"Shhh, shhh!"

" 'where you drink the tea of the breasts of the spinsters of Utica . . .' "

" 'I'm with you in Rockland
>   where we hug and kiss the United States under our
>   bedsheets   the United States that coughs all night
>   and won't let us sleep . . .' "

"What is Rockland?"

"The asylum."

"Shhh, shhh!"

Leo twangs a madhouse apocalypse, bugles the alleluias to a climax of sent up naked innocence. Breaks; sobs.

" 'in my dreams you walk dripping from a sea-journey on the highway across America in tears to the door of my cottage in the Western night' "

Applause, applause.

"What is it about?"

"Love."

"It's what happened to Butterfly's son."

"You are joking?"

"No. You must come and meet them."

My father leads her away. Europa went more willingly with the bull.

"I want a long cool glass of lime with ice to take the taste out of my mouth."

"I'll make you one." Jon takes her towards the house. I back silently and dissolve into shadow. Watch now, watch. Ajax is watching, just outside in the thick shadow beyond the arch. My mother moves away, undulating gently round the fountain. O Galatea, for you it is suddenly thick with merboys, dolphins, horny tritons. Ajax will see it too. Caspar takes her arm. Their words fall into the fountain like tossed coins. She moves again so that his arm is a trident thrust towards her.

"Caspar, Caspar, is that you? You must listen. Jon's got such a marvellous idea for an opera; *Venus and Adonis*, the one you've always wanted to do. He'll write the music and we'll get that marvellous coloured tenor, you know who I mean. You must come and listen right now. Jon's already written some of the overture and it's quite stunning. We'll need a librettist, of course."

"It's the resurrection, man, that's the thing."

They are dragging him towards the house. The piano has been taken in. He half turns smiling apologetically at my mother, hands gesturing his helplessness. She is alone in the courtyard. She pauses. She starts forward. Ajax appears in the arch. Even from here I feel the ripples of her pleasure. I must get closer.

"Darling, I've been trying to get to you all evening. What's the matter? Don't be angry with me."

"You bitch."

"Is it Caspar? I've known him for years. It's only camouflage. Trust me."

"You wrote to him. That wasn't camouflage."

"Wrote to him?"

"And he wrote back something you didn't dare show anyone. You fixed it up between you."

"Darling . . ."

"You tore it up, didn't you?"

"Yes."

"Because of what it said."

"Yes, but that's nothing to do with me."

"His hand on your arm."

"I couldn't just shake it off."

"You wrote to him."

"I didn't."

"I saw it."

"But I didn't."

"What else has been a lie?"

"Darling, don't. I love you, truly. Believe me."

My mother's lover lifts a hand. There is the sharp

stinging sound of a slap; then Ajax turns and runs off through the arch. For a moment she stands quite still. She begins to move forward, a hand outstretched.

"Ajax, Ajax!"

I step out of my arch. "*Ciao*, maman. I think the All-thing's ready to go home. We must say goodnight to Ellie. Were you calling someone?"

Ajax didn't come in the morning. Quite early the police rang my father. The car had been found.

We had walked back. My mother explained that Ajax had already left, unwell. Unwell. The car was gone. Perhaps my mother rang, and again. I kept out of the way.

Ajax had driven off the mole where Gennaro and I had tied up. The water was deep there. An early lone fisherman had seen the car through the clear waves. There was a lot of alcohol in the blood that the sea's tears hadn't been able to wash away. It was thought that Ajax had taken the car to drive back to the Albergo and, in a fit of amnesia, turned left instead of right, downhill instead of up. The car had bucked once on the rocks; the steering wheel folded but the gearshift had stabbed into the groin. After the post mortem the body was buried very quickly. My mother had already left.

I knew exactly how the body would lie as it was carried by the bearers, not straight but like the statue of Shelley in one of the Oxford colleges or the reclining maenad who has passed out of Titian's Bacchanal. It would be quite perfect except for that wound.

" 'Balder is dead. Balder the beautiful. Weep Balder from the power of Hela.' 'Living or dead I loved him not.

Let Hela keep what she hath.' " There was a verdict of accidental death.

We stayed on for a while after the funeral, which only my father attended. There was a lot to do: packing, arrangements. The book was almost finished. My father wrote the summary and Renata typed it. Leo went east to the tour resorts.

I met Gerry in the bar and told her we were leaving.

"That means I'll have to go too. Oh well, I guess it was time to move on."

Ellie and Caspar had gone to Paris taking Jon with them and, I suppose, the children. It had somehow overcast the tourists' summer. Gerry came to see me before we left. She handed me the periscope.

"I brought you this. I didn't know what else to do with it. Jesus, I hope you'll be alright. I worry about you."

I took Gennaro back his grappling hook and rope. No one much noticed my comings and goings now. I'd wanted to keep it, to bury it or throw it into the sea but in the end I just gave it back.

"We are very worried. We don't know if it will be unlucky and drive the fish away." Gennaro crossed himself.

"Oh no, it won't do that."

"One can't tell." He shook his head. "It is said it wasn't an accident."

"The police say . . ."

"What does some little cop know! They want only to keep it quiet and wait for promotion."

I shrugged my shoulders and stood up. "See you." I put out a hand.

"The American girl leaves tomorrow. See you." We shook hands. I don't think I shall see him again. I don't think we shall come to Iticino again.

We are back in London. Fantah has joined us. Renata is still with us hoping to find a husband. We hear Ellie has turned Jon loose. The opera of Venus and Adonis has become a ballet. Caspar will conduct it. Adonis is a young Negro political leader who falls in love with a beautiful middle-aged white woman, wife of a senator. The hounds are his followers who savage him. He staggers dying into an East Ninety-eighth Street dive bar where the owner and *diseuse noire* is versed in black magic and restores him to life. It's to be called *Tammuz and Astarte*. My mother is back.

Often I get out the letters and the periscope: all that remain to become cult objects. One envelope contains a sheet of blank lilac paper. There should be a shrine somewhere for them where others might worship but instead they are my private relics of the only total act I shall ever encounter. My mother's lover has killed Ajax rather than live without the chrysolite. I have made my mythology.

In my mother's eyes I see that she would like to die too but she can't. When spring comes it will hurt her with its brief resurrection. They say the goddess laid her lover's body in a bed of lettuce; that is why the Adonis gardens in their shallow bowls sprang up greenly tall and withered with the festival. "Images of Adonis in wax and terra cotta were placed before the entrance or on the terraces of houses. Women crowded round them or carried them through the town, wailing and beating their breasts with every sign of the deepest grief." Under an arbor of green-ery, in the palace of Arsinoë, Adonis lies on a silver bed. Venus is beside him. Let her seek her lover like Isis through the world, she will not find Ajax again. She will have no more lovers except me. The light on the purple carpet makes her eyes smart. I am my mother's lover now. But I didn't know, I didn't know.

Also by Maureen Duffy available from Virago

THE MICROCOSM

'A highly disturbing and original novel' – *Daily Telegraph*

At the House of Shades, Matt, a bar room philosopher, tries to make sense of the disparate lives which cross here – of Judy who saves herself and her finery for a Saturday night lover, of Steve, the gym teacher who dreads a chance encounter with a pupil in this twilight environment, and of Matt herself, who needs these vicarious exchanges despite the security of her relationship with Rae and her sense that this lesbian sanctuary is a prison too, enforcing the guilt and estrangement of the city streets beyond. Elsewhere there are women such as Mare, trapped within an unwanted marriage and unable to admit her sexuality, and Cathy, for whom the discovery that she is not 'the only one in the world' is an affirmation of her existence. With its innovative structure and style, perfectly mirroring the voices and experiences of women forced by society to live on the margins, *The Microcosm* remains as powerful today as when originally published in 1966.

THAT'S HOW IT WAS

'[She] creates the world of her childhood and adolescence so that one can feel, smell, and taste it' – *Doris Lessing*

Paddy is illegitimate, the daughter of yet another Paddy, Irish and IRA who abandons her English mother, Louey, at birth. This is the story of that mother – frail but with an indomitable spirit – of that daughter and of their life together, seen through the clear eyes of Paddy as a child and as an adolescent. Set in wartime England, wonderfully evoking working-class life of that period, the subtle changing relationship between Paddy and Louey is movingly conveyed in a novel which is really a love story, but this time telling of the love between parent and child.

Also available in the Lesbian Landmarks series

POISON FOR TEACHER
Nancy Spain

'An inspired craziness rules . . . Miss Spain has yet to write a better book' – *Elizabeth Bowen*

A nasty attack of murder has broken out at Radcliff Hall (aka Roedean) which brings, in the unlikely guise of schoolteachers, two most unorthodox detectives – revue star Miriam Birdseye (aka Hermione Gingold) and her Russian ballerina chum Natasha Nerkovina – hotfoot to solve it. Undaunted by the horrors of matron, mutton, Bally Netball and the pupils' endless recitals of *Innisfree* ('Ai will araise and go now . . .') Birdseye *et cie* triumph once more.

Poison for Teacher, first published in 1949, is one of Nancy Spain's most exuberant performances in the genre which she made triumphantly her own: novels of detection generously laced with comedy and high camp.

Nancy Spain, journalist, novelist and panellist on television programmes such as *What's My Line?* and *Juke Box Jury*, was one of the most witty and lovable figures in post-war Britain.

WINTER LOVE
Han Suyin

'A stunning novel – resonant, penetrating and unsentimental'
– *Georgina Hammick*

Red is a married woman with children. But since adolescence she has been desperate to conceal from herself and others the true significance of her feelings for women. Now, with middle-age approaching fast, her thoughts turn insistently to her student days in that bitterly cold winter of the last year of the war when Mara offered – and Red rejected – love, desire, and trust. Painfully, Red relives the past, and comes to see the part that cruelty, loss and fear have played in the formation of her frozen sexuality. And with enlightenment, comes the possibility of thaw . . . .

Han Suyin, born in China in 1917, is best known for her novel *A Many Splendoured Thing*, and for her volumes of autobiography. *Winter Love*, her beautifully written and perceptive novel, was first published in 1962.

THE CHILD MANUELA
Christa Winsloe

The novel of the film *Schoolgirls in Uniform*

Manuela von Meinhardis has a loving mother and a callous, egotistical father, an officer in a crack Prussian regiment. On her mother's death Manuela is sent to a repressive school for officers' daughters where all affection is outlawed. The harshness of the regime reflects the iron fist of Prussianism and the Hitlerism already well entrenched by 1932 when Winsloe was writing: the cruelties practised by female staff upon their pupils foreshadow the complicities and horrors of Nazism. In such an environment, only Fräulein von Bernburg offers tenderness and love, and for that both she and Manuela must suffer.

Available in Britain for the first time in more than half a century, *The Child Manuela* is the remarkable and passionate novel on which the famous film *Schoolgirls in Uniform* was based.

A FAVOURITE OF THE GODS
Sybille Bedford

'A writer of remarkable accomplishment' – *Evelyn Waugh*

One autumn in the late 1920s, a beautiful woman boards a train on the Italian riviera. Her name is Constanza, and she is *en route* to Brussels and a new marriage. With her is her young daughter Flavia, who is going to England for the education she has always wanted. An odd, almost meaningless incident interrupts their journey, and Constanza makes a seemingly abrupt and casual decision that changes the course of both their lives. Yet perhaps the pattern had already been set by Constanza's own mother, the American heiress Anna, who years before had left home for a strange marriage with an Italian prince . . .